Bodymore Kingpins

Lock Down Publications and Ca$h
Presents

Bodymore Kingpins

A Novel by *Romell Tukes*

Lock Down Publications
Po Box 944
Stockbridge, Ga 30281

Visit our website @
www.lockdownpublications.com

First Edition January 2023
Printed in the United States of America

Lock Down Publications
Like our page on Facebook: Lock Down Publications @
www.facebook.com/lockdownpublications.ldp
Book interior design by: **Shawn Walker**
Edited by: **Jill Alicea**

Stay Connected with Us!

Text **LOCKDOWN** to 22828 to stay up-to-date with new releases, sneak peaks, contests and more…
Thank you.

Submission Guideline.

Submit the first three chapters of your completed manuscript to ldpsubmissions@gmail.com, subject line: Your book's title. The manuscript must be in a .doc file and sent as an attachment. Document should be in Times New Roman, double spaced and in size 12 font. Also, provide your synopsis and full contact information. If sending multiple submissions, they must each be in a separate email.

Have a story but no way to send it electronically? You can still submit to LDP/Ca$h Presents. Send in the first three chapters, written or typed, of your completed manuscript to:

LDP: Submissions Dept
Po Box 944
Stockbridge, Ga 30281

DO NOT send original manuscript. Must be a duplicate.

Provide your synopsis and a cover letter containing your full contact information.

Thanks for considering LDP and Ca$h Presents.

Chapter 1
Big Sandy Federal Prison, KY

Rags rushed out of his unit, A-4, in his gray sweat suit and white Air Force Ones sneakers to chill with his boys Crown and Fly from Baltimore. Summertime in Kentucky felt like a desert but Rags didn't mind he loved the heat.

Inmates of all races flooded the yard on this nice day: Mexicans who ran with the MS-13 gang, white boys with racist tattoos on their face who called themselves AC, and your regular Bloods and Crips gang members. Rags was neutral, so he ran with the Baltimore cats.

The feds were very different from the state because you have to run with a car in the feds. A car consists of your state, gang, or the region you were down with just in case a war breaks out. Most inmates in the USP like Big Sandy had a lot of time or had fucked up in another prison like Rags did.

Being from Baltimore, Maryland, he made sure he put on for his city, especially around D.C. niggas who they ran with in the feds because they only had one state prison Supermax. Three years ago, he was sentenced to a five-year bid on a drug indictment, but since it was his first charge and the feds only had Rags on wiretap, they couldn't get him how the government truly wanted. Rags took the five years at the age of seventeen and now he was twenty years old, on his way out the door. The government tried to portray Rags as the top plug in Baltimore under two other individuals they were still looking into, but they didn't have enough evidence for the state, so they charged Rags with some weak shit.

"Yo, Rags, what up, son? I need to holla at you, son," an old gangsta named OG Chuck from New York shouted when Rags walked through the gates on the yard.

"What's up, Unc?"

"Your little man Rob still owes me five bands for that little shit I gave him and my patience is running thin. I can send my little wolves at him, but I like you," OG Chuck said with his smooth, deep voice. OG Chuck was the shot caller for the New York car and had a few life sentences and was very respected all over.

"I'ma have my young boys handle that, yo, I got you," Rags told him.

"That's why I like you, son." OG Chuck walked off.

A few people stopped Rags on his way to Crown and Fly to talk about dumb shit that was taking place in their units with his homies owing money.

"What's up shawty?" Crown said with the Baltimore accent they all had, including Rags.

"Ain't shit, yo. Came out to fuck with y'all broke-ass niggas," Rags joked, sitting down on a bench near the basketball court.

"You used to be that nigga, young'un. Your ass broke now," Fly said, laughing.

"Nigga, you never touched a key or sold a gram. For all I know, you could have been a vicious smoker." Rags got on his boy Fly's ass, almost making Crown die in laughter.

"Everybody from West Baltimore knows about me, shawty. I ain't get seventy years for sitting down watching my uncle or brother get chicken, little nigga." Fly took a shot because Rags' brother and uncle were the real plugs in the city.

"When my mom and dad were out free, they had the whole city East to West. My bloodline is all breadwinners," Rags shot back.

"Your dad used to supply me and my whole family before he got knocked," Crown stated.

"Your dad and mom are legends, little nigga. You not, shawty," Fly stated.

"I'm an upcoming king," Rags boasted as he tied his long dreads in a ponytail.

Rags stood six feet tall, brown-skinned with a nice lean frame that drove women crazy. Even a few female correctional officers were on his body.

"Yo shawty, you from southeast, we from the west. Shit is different - the money and crime rate," Crown stated.

"Hold on, bro. Perkins Homes will always have southeast in a chokehold," Fly stated.

"I heard Polo taking over that shit," Crown said with a dislike for the man who had put his brother in a wheelchair and got his sister murdered in broad daylight.

"When I touch down, I'm taking over the whole city, yo, on some Wall Street bully shit. Watch."

"It's not the same as three years ago when your parents was out," Crown said as Rags walked off, into his own thoughts, thinking how it was before he came to jail.

Chapter 2
Southeast, Baltimore
Three years prior

Rags did a spin move and cut through two players making a layup.

"Step y'all game up," Rags stated, making his way up to the top so he could get the ball again.

Rags had come out to the local park near Perkins Homes, where he grew up loved. His grandmom still lived there, but his parents had moved out a few years back.

"Pass me the ball, yo," a kid named Kanno yelled. He was best friends with Rags.

When Rags passed Kanno the ball, he took the open shot on a three-point line and missed it with an air ball.

"Damn, my nigga!" another kid named Preme shouted.

"It's cool. We still up, shawty!" Kanno yelled, knowing he fucked up.

Now since it was the other team's ball, Rags played defensive as his opponent had fast dribbles, but he was on him.

The kid missed the shot and Rags got the ball and took it back from the top. He hit a three-pointer, putting them up. Rags' team needed one more shot, so he passed it to Fat P, who had not scored all day. Fat P didn't have nobody to guard him because everybody thought he was trash. Fat P took the shot and made it, all net, surprising the whole court, even sideline lookers.

"Ok, cuz." Kanno slapped his cousin Fat P on the ass for showing good sportsmanship.

"You know how I do, yo." Fat P felt like the man.

"That's your dad, Rags?" Kanno asked, seeing a white Bentley coupe GT pull up to the park with the top down.

"Yeah. I'ma see y'all next week." Rags took his ball and ran to his dad.

"Call me later!" Kanno shouted.

Rags and Kanno had been best of friends since he was a young kid. He remembered the night Baltimore police killed his parents in

Perkins Homes. Since then, Kanno's grandmom had been taking care of him.

Climbing inside the car, he saw his dad give him a look, and Rags knew what that meant to take off his dirty sneakers so he wouldn't fuck up the rugs.

"How was it, my son?" Proof, his father, asked in a smooth voice that had a Barry White sound.

"Fun. I won/"

"We," his dad corrected him.

"Huh?" Rags seemed confused.

"You won with your team. A man is only as strong as his team" Proof schooled his son, something he did daily.

"Okay. I understand, Dad."

"Hope so. You will always be a boss, but you need to work with others to be a bigger boss," Proof said, getting on the highway to head home.

"How did you become a boss, Dad?"

"Hard work and a lot of failed attempts in life."

"A lot of losses, basically?" asked Rags, getting the point.

"I went through losses just so you don't have to - none of my kids will. Look at Fatima, your sister, starting college/ Your older brother Sunny opened a car lot. And me with the stores. You next up," Proof said, seeing Rags smile from ear to ear.

"I'm ready."

"We gonna see. You never know when you will have to step up one day." Proof drove into PG county, far away from Baltimore and closer to D.C.

When they arrived at the mansion, four luxury cars were parked out front. There was a three car garage and a beautiful land-scape. Inside, there were five bedrooms, four bathrooms, an indoor gym, studio, game room, basement, two-level guest house in the back, a pool, and a small basketball court.

Rags grew up in the projects but five years ago, his family moved and started to open businesses. He was told his family hit the lotto, but that was far from the truth. But Rags was still a kid, so they placed the wool over his eyes for now.

***

West Baltimore

Sunny posted up outside of an abandoned warehouse for his guests to arrive so they could start their Monday meeting. Sunny was a young kingpin under his father and uncle following their footsteps. Controlling a small part of the Westside on a block called Eden Street, he was seeing over $100,000 a week on a bad day all off of dope, a.k.a. dog food. His dad Proof had the whole city in a chokehold beside his two rivals X and HD, who hated the Scott family with a passion. Sunny and his uncle Five were in the streets while Proof played the back field and controlled the business aspect of shit.

At age twenty-one, Sunny felt like he had everything in front of him already laid out in the open. Sunny had recently opened a car lot in West Baltimore near one of his dad's tire and rim shops.

Two unmarked cars pulled up and his guests hopped out in regular clothes, but they were both undercover cops. One detective was Sunny's uncle Dozen, the dirtiest cop in B-more. Niggas feared Dozen because he was both a street nigga and a cop.

"Nephew," Dozen said, tucking in the federal badge hanging from his neck.

"What's up, Unc and Whitey?" Sunny spoke, also addressing the other cop whom they called Whitey because he was a dirty white boy.

"Sunny, I hear you out here doing your thing," Whitey stated trying to get in the good spirit with Sunny so he could up their pay.

"Doing me. But my dad wants to know about X and HD because word is they trying to team up on us?" Sunny saw his uncle's surprised face because this was new to him.

"I ain't heard shit like that, shawty," Dozen said.

"I'ma keep my ears open," Whitey added, writing it down.

"One last thing: did you ever find out who the insider was?" Sunny asked his uncle Dozen, who nodded his head.

"What's he talking about, Dozen?" Whitey asked nervously.

Dozen didn't even reply. He pulled out a used handgun and Sunny pulled out a Glock 19, both aiming at Whitey.

"We let you eat and you got hungry, cracker. The night our spot got robbed, you was the first cop on the scene which seemed weird because you was off that night," Sunny said, speaking about the loss he recently took.

"Sunny, this is all force, man, I swear!" Whitey cried out.

"I lost two good men and a lot of product. You backtracked to make sure the killer did the job correctly. All I have to ask is who was it and who sent them?" Sunny asked, seeing Whitey look at Dozen for help. But his ex-partner had a gun pressed to his head.

"X sent them. It was Sean P and some other young kid I never saw," Whitey stated.

Boom! Boom! Boom! Boom!

Sunny and Dozen both killed the cop and dragged his body into a small swampy area, knowing he would be found any day now. But this was the punishment for betrayal.

Chapter 3
University of Maryland

Fatimah already liked her new college. It was a large campus with dorms and a bunch of brick buildings. At first, she was going to go to a school in North Carolina, but her family requested her to stay close.

Being a freshman at college was hard itself, but having to meet new people had to be the worst part of it all, she thought. Fatimah was taking up criminal justice so she could become a police officer and serve her country some way. With some much shit going on in the world from police killings, police killing innocent civilians, riots, protests all over the world, and the unfair justice system, Fatimah felt as if it was her calling.

Growing up in Baltimore she saw a lot in her young years from killing, drug sales, and all types of crazy violence until her parents sent Fatimah and her brothers to private school for a better chance at opportunity. Seeing everything made her strong and grateful for what she did have and what she wanted to do with herself.

"You new here?" A white chick approached Fatimah in a textbook store. A long line wrapped all through the store and outside of it.

"Yes I am. My name is Fatimah."

"I'm Lindsey. I'm from Utah."

"Utah, wow!"

"Yes. I've been at this school three years, but it's my last. Then I can become a federal agent, or at least take the test," Lindsey said, smiling.

"That's great! I'm looking forward to becoming a cop."

"Oh, how crazy! Your major is criminal justice then, right?" asked Lindsey, standing in line with Fatimah.

"Yes. I can't wait! How are the professors here?"

"Well, they are mostly cool."

"Can't wait. I'm from Maryland, so I figured this would be a good choice."

"I wanted to attend Georgetown in Washington, D.C. this year for my last go around." Lindsey waved at a few students she knew from last year's classes.

"I've heard that is a good school."

"Totally. What dorm are you in? I'm in B-C 4 next to the library building," said Fatimah, looking at a piece of paper with the room location written down.

"Oh shit, that's my dorm! What floor?" Lindsey was extra surprised because she had never seen Fatimah, although the school was very big with a lot of students.

"Four."

"Shitting me! In what room? I'm on the fourth also in room 412," Lindsey added.

"I'm 415, across the hall."

"We can chill together. Do you have a roommate?" asked Lindsey.

"Nah, not yet. How about you?"

"I had one for three years, but she graduated two months ago, thank God!"

"How was she?"

"OMG, that bitch was dirty and nasty, sleeping with every man on campus. No lie she had to fuck a new guy every night, I swear," Lindsey stated in disgust.

Fatimah stood five-five, thick in all the right places, cocoa brown skin, hazel eyes, real long curly hair, and a smile to die for.

"Fuck her! Everything about her screamed bitch and I heard her family in Texas were all racists. I hate people like that," Lindsey huffed.

"I feel the same, Lindsey."

The two of them talked and chilled all day and even went to get a cup of coffee from Starbucks.

***

Downtown Baltimore

Five lived in a nice condo apartment in the downtown section away from the slums and projects where he grew up. Being in the Scott family held a lot of weight in B-more because their bloodline dated back from their great-grandfather, who killed two state troopers and died in prison.

Five was Proof's younger brother, but he was the family face of the Scott empire. At twenty-five years old, life couldn't be better for the young man, who drove fancy cars, wore a lot of jewelry, new clothes, and fucked the baddest chicks.

Proof was supposed to come over sometime today to go over details for the next order and more business plans. Sunny was laying low in D.C. until the heat with Whitey died down because the city police department had been cracking down.

Dozen said everything would be back to normal in a few days. The department knew Whitey was a piece of shit. His death went very unnoticed to some, but Whitey's aunty and cousin worked, there so they made a big issue about the unsolved murder.

The door buzzer rang and he went to answer it, already knowing who it was: his big brother, whom he loved to death. Since they were kids, Proof and Five had been close, even when they used to go around robbing niggas just to put food in the house. Growing up, they had a big family scattered all through B-more and New York as well, where they got all their drugs.

"Yo, what's up, big bro? I miss you, yo," Five stated, embracing Proof.

"You look like hell, yo. You been fucking with that coke again?" asked Proof, knowing his bro was dipping and dapping in sniffing coke.

"Nah, why you say that?" Five looked to his left, lying.

"Nigga, your ass lying! I see shit dripping out your nose. But I ain't come here for that. We got a small issue."

"What is it? Everything is still going down, right?" Five needed his work because his clients had been dry for two days now, and today made three.

"Yes, but they not coming to us. We gotta go to them."

"Sunny in D.C.," Five said.

Proof looked at him like he had lost his fucking mind. "I'm not sending my son up there. You going up there to get it. Drive with a white bitch in different cars, and everything better be there," Proof stated, leaving, not even mentioning the $170,000 Five owed him from his last fuck up.

Chapter 4
Downtown Baltimore

ReRe ran the rim and tire shops when her husband went outta town on business. Someone had to hold it down. With four shops all over the city, she stayed busy handling financial sheets, meetings, customer service, employment, and the daily gross. Not only was ReRe a pretty face and body, but she was well-educated with a Bachelor's degree in Business Management. In her late thirties, ReRe still looked better than any bitch in B-more. She favored Beyonce Knowles with her gold complexion, golden curly natural hair, hazel eyes, and thick curves.

She met her husband when in school and fell in love. Proof gave her the world even when he did not have a dime. The love they shared was different, it was unconditional and genuine. She had only been with one other man, but ReRe never did nothing sexual with him.

Proof took her heart and popped her cherry and since then, it was no turning back. ReRe's parents hated Proof so much that when their daughter got pregnant, they gave her an option to get an abortion and leave Proof alone or get out of their home. ReRe packed her bags and left with no problem, moving in with Proof at his aunty's house in the basement. Having her first child Sunny was the best thing that ever happened to her and Proof. Once the baby was born, ReRe started working 9 to 5 just to pay the bills and so they could eventually get their own spot. Months later, everything changed and Proof got into a jam in New York and got sent to Rikers Island for a year.

When he came out, he found a construction job and moved his family into Perkins Homes where he grew up and built a name for himself, but Proof's family name was already established in Baltimore city. After a few years, ReRe and Proof had Fatimah and Rags, then shit started getting real. Two jobs wasn't getting everything done, so Proof took a trip to New York again to visit some family and their life changed.

"How much is some twenty-two-inch rims?" A young black kid with gold teeth asked.

"For what type of car?" ReRe asked, about to leave and let the manager take over because she was only there going over bills.

"A Benz coupe." The young kid flashed a smile, thinking he was doing something because he was selling a little work around town. But the young man didn't know her son Sunny was supplying him and his whole block.

"I don't think putting rims on a Benz is a something to do. Luxury cars are meant to ride factory. It makes the car classy and makes you look more like a boss," ReRe stated.

"Hahaha, I been a boss, beautiful."

"Sorry, playa." ReRe laughed at him, gathering her purse and car keys to leave.

"What you driving, a Honda?" the kid joked thinking ReRe was a regular bad broke bitch: the three B's she looked down on.

"I used to." She wasn't in denial

"Oh, so you don't know nothing about luxury. Better yet, maybe a manager can help me," he said, going hard in the shop.

"Well, for your information, I used to drive a Honda. Now I'm pushing that two-tone Rolls Royce Wraith outside that you're parked next to and I own the shop. Any more questions?" ReRe stunted on the kid.

He felt like shit. The young thug turned to leave with his head down as ReRe and the manager died laughing before she made her way to the next location.

***

Baltimore Private School

Rags disliked school, but he was very liked and known throughout the place. Everybody from teachers, students, and even the janitor knew his name. Being in high school for any kid could be rough with bullies and troublemakers, but Rags held an image. Most people thought by sending their children to private school it would be a lot better than any public school, but boy, that was a lie.

The rich kids in private school could get away with murder if their parents had a few dollars or even a known name.

It was lunchtime and Rags was sitting at the table with his crew, laughing and joking, when his high school crush walked inside with four of her girls.

"There go Carena," one of his boys stated, tapping him on the shoulder.

"I know, nigga, chill," Rags replied nervously, thinking about the high school dance coming up.

Carena was the same age as him, but due to how smart she was, the school skipped her a few grades, so this was Carena's last year. Carena's mom was a white woman and her father was a strong black man who raised his daughter correctly.

Rags stared at Carena, but when she caught his eye contact, he quickly turned his head.

Everybody wanted Carena in the school, from the older dudes to the younger ones, because she was one of the baddest chicks in school. Carena was high yellow, short, with long curly hair, a perfect smile, and nice lips, which he loved. She never gave any boy a second of her time, so most assumed she had to be gay or weird.

Looking back at her table not too far away, Rags built up the courage to go ask Carena if she would come to the school dance. Walking over there felt like the walk of death in slow motion.

Once at the table, to his surprise, Carena spoke first, calling Rags by his real name. "Hey Doug," Carena said, smiling at him.

"What's up, Carena, how you been?" he asked, trying to remember why he was standing there in the first place.

"Same ole. You haven't spoken to me in about three months. I thought we was cool," Carena said, remembering the last time he said hi was when they had seen each other in the school library.

"Sorry, been a little busy." Rags' hands were starting to sweat, so he wiped them on his pants.

"Okay, cool. Well, I'll see you around, I guess." She stood to leave with her girls as the next period bell rang.

Rags' mental started to race, seeing he was running outta time to shoot his only shot at her. "Can I take you to the school dance?"

Rags shot out so fast that it sounded like he was speaking Chinese or some other foreign language.

Carena stood there for a few seconds staring at him, but really looking through Rags, in her own deep thought. "Why me?" she asked.

"I can't see myself asking nobody else and I really like you." Rags couldn't believe the words that came outta his mouth.

"You serious?"

"Yes."

"You want to be my boyfriend? Because I really like you too." She blushed. Carena had a crush on him too.

"I do."

"So we official now, boyfriend and girlfriend." Carena smiled at her new boyfriend as Rags walked her to class, feeling like a playa.

Chapter 5
East B-more

Sunny drove around in his all-black truck with presidential tints, riding, thinking, and smoking a fifth of exotic weed. The other night one of his close friends' bodies was found with a X marked on his forehead from a branding.

Once he heard the word X, all thoughts went to his top rival X, a man whom his father Proof also hated with a passion. The beef with the Scott family and X went back from when X and Proof were kids. Word on the street was that Proof killed X brother and shit been a war since it wasn't so much over turf as most thought the bloodshed was really personal. Now the beef was up to Sunny and his crew.

Driving down East Baltimore, Sunny saw a familiar face coming out of an abandoned house near Dallas street.

Sunny spun the block and parked on a dark block to make sure his mind was not playing tricks on him.

***

Dragon came out one of his traps with a book bag, about to meet up with one of his young boys to drop off some dope he sold for his uncle X, one of the biggest dope boys in B-more. At nineteen, Dragon loved the fast life. He only wished he could have made better choices because two weeks ago, Dragon did something bad. While driving back from VA where he was selling drugs behind his uncle's back, Dragon got pulled over. Dragon got arrested for fourteen kilos of dope and a Draco, but Dragon got released and was told to report straight to the Baltimore police department. Not wasting one extra second, Dragon went directly to the police station and told them everything he knew about X's organization, not missing a peep. Ratting on his uncle was foul, but Dragon knew he had to do what he had to do for his sake, his girlfriend, and his newborn. He still thought he was a solid street nigga because he would bust his gun at any given moment.

Walking across the street, talking on the phone to his ex about the money she stole from him, Dragon wasn't paying any mind to the street while crossing. A black SUV ran right into him, knocking him off his feet.

"What the fuck?" Dragon groaned, in serious pain, trying to move.

The driver hoped out of the SUV as if he was a helping civilian. "You okay, sir?" the man dressed in all black asked. He was wearing a rope chain with gold teeth and gangsta braids, a Baltimore thing, which is to rock your braids to the side.

"Fuck your bitch ass, nigga!" he cried in discomfort.

"Caught your ass now." Sunny pulled out a gun, aiming at Dragon's head.

When Dragon saw Sunny, he tried to crawl away in fear of his life being snatched by the grim reaper.

Bloc! Bloc! Bloc!

Sunny put all three bullets in Dragon's skull, killing him in the middle of the street he was born on.

***

Eastside B-more
Next day

X blew weed smoke in the air of a back room of an apartment building his girlfriend owned. X had a lot of real estate around town, which was his side hustle, and his wifey Jena was a top real estate agent.

The news of his nephew being murdered in the middle of one of his blocks made X furious. Nobody besides one group of people were crazy enough to touch anything X loved besides the Scott family he hated.

Although B Dragon was a killer, he was smarter than most because he knew how to get money and stand on loyalty, so X valued that overall. Hearing he got killed saddened his heart even though Dragon understood what came with the street life.

Going against Proof, Five, and Sunny was hard because they had a strong army and the police force on their side, so they had power. Warring with Proof took a lot of time and he lost a lot of men and money, but in the end, everything was worth it because Proof killed X's brother and best friend years ago.

X was the type to hold grudges against any enemy, and he wasn't the only one who wanted Proof and his family dead. There was also a man named HD who had lived in B-more his whole life mostly, but he was born in Washington, D.C., a city where everybody looked up to killers like Wayne Perry.

Proof and HD's beef started around the same time as X's beef, so the city had a high crime rate, thanks to all three crews going back to back for years. X loved to get money and had his own army, but lately he had been thinking about teaming up with HD, a man he saw only a few times, but X knew more muscle could be useful. Selling keys of dope where X lived on the eastside for years, his big brother Lip became one of the city's biggest heroin suppliers until Proof killed him. Most people wouldn't even believe X was a kingpin because of his looks, style, and the way he carried himself. The streets called him X because he looked like a dark-skinned version of Malcom X with glasses. X rocked expensive suits and spoke very calm and low. His wife Jena knew about her husband's life because X put her on to a bag, buying her homes to flip and sell, building her name up in the real estate field.

X checked the time. He had somewhere to be, so he left the low-key crib with his nephew on his mind. X had to stop by his sister's crib to comfort her and bring her some money and mourn over their loss.

Chapter 6
Southeast Baltimore

Getting ready for school had to be the hardest thing for Kanno, whose real name was Kennedy Jackson, to do in the morning. Not only did he have to get himself ready, but also his little sister Egyptian, who was only a year younger than him but went to the same school as Kanno.

Normally his mom CeCe would be out smoking crack and shooting dope somewhere in the projects or asleep, and waking her up was dangerous. Their mom had been smoking crack since before their time, but back in the day, CeCe used to be a getting money bad bitch until she met her children's father Sin.

When CeCe met Sin, she thought he was the sweetest young man from the way he made love to her, talked, cared, and treated CeCe until one day his other side showed. CeCe heard from other people in the hood that Sin did drugs and abused women, but CeCe was also struck by love until one day he struck her.

CeCe never did drugs until the night Sin put a gun to her head, forcing her to shoot heroin and smoke crack with him, not caring she was pregnant with Kanno's older brother Nice. By the time Nice was born, CeCe was a full-blown fiend and Sin had her turning tricks, even when CeCe became pregnant with Kanno. Life felt like hell and heaven at the same time for CeCe, and even after giving birth to Kanno, the party didn't stopped. Sin was going around robbing local drug dealers and became a big target. The night their third baby Egyptian was born, Sin couldn't make it to the hospital because he was kidnapped in retaliation by some big-time drug dealer he robbed named HD. Days after Egyptian's birth, CeCe was worried to death about Sin.

One evening, detectives came knocking on CeCe's door to inform her that Sin's body was found in a river with his hands cut off. Ever since that day, CeCe had been going hard on drugs, not given a fuck about her kids or own life or well-being. Last year, her oldest son Nice was sentenced to life in the feds for killing an undercover cop during a drug bust. Nice had no clue the man was the police because he planned to rob him and take the four keys of dope he claimed he was going to pay for just so the man could bring the drugs so he could rob him. Nice killed him before he could say who he was: an undercover officer. The words didn't escape his mouth.

Kanno got himself dressed. Luckily, he had taken a shower last night so he could just head straight to school. He was up on the house phone all night with his best friend Rags, talking about their favorite ball players in the NBA. When Rags lived in the same projects, they used to spend the night at each other's house daily and walk to school together, but now shit was different.

Walking into the dirty kitchen, he saw Egyptian dressed, eating a bowl of grits because that was all they had until the EBT money came in a few days.

"You ready?" he asked.

"You?" she shot back, showing her young pretty face.

"After school, we both gonna clean up around here." Kanno looked around in disgust seeing beer bottles and used needles.

"Okay." Egyptian went to get her book bag so they could walk up the block to school.

***

Downtown Baltimore

Proof, Sunny, and his brother Five all came to one of the rim and tire shops to meet up so they could discuss business and future investments.

"Sunny, you and Dozen did good on that cop situation. I got a lot of respect for you young'uns, but the next situation ain't gonna be so easy," Proof told his son.

"I'm ready," Sunny assured him.

Since being in the game, Proof put his son through the craziest tests, from testing his loyalty to killing one of Sunny's own close friends, who ratted to the local police about the family business after they let him in the ranks.

"You know X gonna be on us until he gets back at us," Five said, pouring himself a glass of Patron.

"What does that mean?" Proof didn't give a fuck at all what X did or had planned.

"Let's focus on this money," Sunny added, not caring about the war, just the money, because his young boys wanted to eat.

"The drugs aren't the issue. Sunny, y'all holding down the blocks and projects is what matters and upping the manpower. The key to winning a war is following the art of war, so this is what we gonna do. Five, you and your Piru homies keep an eye on X and if possible, kill everything he loves," Proof stated.

Five was a big homie of the Blood set called Piru, which was the biggest gang in B-more, and Five had an army of soldiers at his disposal at any second.

"I'm on it, brother. My little niggas know what time it is, plus X people killed a capo last summer, so niggas want blood," Five said.

"I want in," Sunny said.

"No, I need you to focus on HD and the money aspect," Proof said. "Remember, you still fresh off the porch, son. You jumped right into the big boy league overnight." Proof made all of them laugh.

"The shipment should be there soon. Let's cross our fingers and hope Five do the right things. If not, his ass on the chopping block," Proof said seriously, and the crew all knew it.

Chapter 7
Baltimore Private H.S.

Tonight was the big night and everybody came out to the school dance fresh to death. Rags' father had bought him a clean Gucci suit with shoes to match and Proof bought Kanno and Fat P fly suits to rock. Proof knew how close the gang was so he always tried to help out. Proof went way back with Kanno's and Fat P's families growing up.

"Yo, this shit is nice, yo," Rags said, looking around inside of the school gym, which was hooked up with flashing lights, a DJ booth, and tables.

"This the last dance, bro. I'm glad they let us in your school this year," Kanno said because last year, the private school didn't allow kids from other schools to come until a parent filed a lawsuit.

"I like your school," Fat P said, looking around at all the different races there. It was unlike his public school, which was majority African-American.

"There she go." Rags grabbed both of his friends when Carena walked through the doors in a white dress with heels followed by six other young girls.

"Who the first chick?" Kanno thought Carena was a model.

"Word, yo, she bad as fuck. Rags, you can never get nothing like that," Fat P joked as Carena and her girls walked right up to Rags.

"Hey Doug," Carena said, checking him out and liking his attire.

"You look nice," Rags replied, blushing.

"Thanks." Carena took a look at Rags' friends and could tell neither one of them went to the school.

Kanno and Fat P looked at each other in shock that Rags even knew the beautiful young woman who was his girlfriend.

"Let's go have fun and my boys can dance with your friends," Rags suggested, seeing both of his friends were scared because all of Carena girls were seniors and dimes.

"Let's do it," Carena said, and the night started as they all danced for hours.

Later that night, Carena offered to take Rags and his boys home, but he declined, not wanting her to know where they lived and where he grew up.

Carena ended the night giving him a lip-to-lip kiss, fucking his head up, but Rags planned to remember the night forever. He would never forget the look on his boys' faces when he told them she was his wifey.

***

Baltimore, Maryland

On the outskirts of the city laid nice homes from middle class to upper class, and Carena lived in the middle class. Her dad was a cop and her mom was a nurse, both of whom were strict on their only daughter ,who had a bright future.

Carena was in her room with Jade, her best friend, who had been close to Carena since the first grade.

"You really like that kid?" asked Jade outta nowhere.

"Who, Doug?" Carena responded, looking in her mirror, doing her hair and listening to music.

"Yes, dummy. I mean, he cute and all, but he young."

"Jade, he's the same age as us."

"You know what I mean. You about to go off to college and he will still be in high school." Jade tried to open her girl's eyes.

"In high school with you. He's a good person, plus I've liked him since I laid eyes on him, Jade, so you can stop," Carena defended her boyfriend because she really liked him.

"Do you even know where he lives, anything about him, his family?"

"No. I do know his family is rich or something. His dad comes to pick him up in that nice car"

"What if he's a serial killer?" Jade's eyes widened.

Carena knew her bestie always took shit to the highest level. "Who, Doug?"

"Yes. He looks cold-blooded."

"Jade, shut up and let's go to the mall." Carena got dressed, paying Jade no mind as she thought about the kiss she shared with Rags last night.

***

West Baltimore

Five had just come from a meeting with his crew, alerting them about the ongoing war he planned to turn up a notch, and everybody was aboard. A new member to Five's crew told him HD was fucking with some little bitch outta the eastside of B-more, so he wanted to deliver that info to Sunny, who awaited him at a nearby gas station.

At the gas station, he saw Sunny's truck parked with the lights on. Five hated coming out on this side of town too late because HD's people had a few blocks around the corner, so it was dangerous.

"You like playing with fire, don't you, young nigga?" Five said, climbing in Sunny's SUV, looking around.

"What you mean, yo?" Sunny had no clue as to what his uncle was talking about.

"This HD turf."

"Fuck that nigga," Sunny spit back with a loaded gun on his lap off safety.

"You must not care for your life, but I got the drop on HD."

"Now we talking." Sunny rubbed his palms, glad Five ain't called him to talk about no dumb shit.

"HD got a young hood rat bitch by the name of Roseia a few blocks over next door to that Jamaican store Growth got killed at." Five missed his boy Growth. He was a getting money nigga down with Five's Piru gang, but he got caught in the wrong hood one night and got killed in front of his daughter.

"Roseia," Sunny repeated as if the name sounded familiar. Then it hit him. Back in middle school, Roseia gave him and his crew head under the school bleachers and her shit was fire.

"Yeah. He should be there tonight. My little homie paid Roseia to line up the hit for you."

"You sure your homie got the correct info?" Sunny wanted to make sure because he disliked killing innocent people.

"Do I question you?"

"At times. But this shit ain't personal. I hit targets not bystanders." Sunny looked at his uncle, who knew what Sunny was getting at.

"You getting real big headed and them two people I killed was in the wrong place at the wrong time." Five referred to a shootout he had two months ago with X's people. A fifteen-year-old girl got killed along with an elderly lady trying to cross the street.

"I'll call you when it's done."

"Don't call me, little nigga. Call your father. And Dozen looking for you."

Five got out of the SUV, shaking his head.

Chapter 7
Maryland University College

Fatima walked out of her class with an hour to spare and wanted to get some French vanilla cappuccino from the college cafe so she could get an energy boost before her next class three buildings over.

This weekend coming up, Lindsey invited her to an on-campus party, but Fatima had some school work so she respectfully declined. Partying wasn't Fatima's thing, even though she liked to have fun. There were a ton of things to do besides smoke, drink, and have sex. Fatima didn't smoke or drink and sex was out of the question, so sticking to her books was all the fun she needed at the moment.

"Excuse me." A young man approached her near an exit.

"Yes?" Fatima replied, trying to get out of the building, but the young man was somewhat in her way.

"I saw you in English class this morning and the poem you did was good. Not too many people know you remixed Maya Angelo." The kid caught Fatima by surprise.

Fatima had a class assignment to write a poem and read it in front of the class and she hated poems. That was her weak point. So Fatima took a poem from a famous poet and remixed it, putting her own twist on it.

"Thanks, I guess." Fatima felt somewhat embarrassed .

"What's your name?" He moved out of the way so Fatima could walk and followed her on campus.

"Fatima."

"Oh, like Prophet Muhammad's first daughter?" he asked, knowing a lot about religions.

"Yes, how did you know?" Fatima's dad was a Muslim so he named her after the last messenger of Allah's daughter.

"My family is Muslim, but I'm not. I just grew up studying religion for my own beliefs," he said as Fatima nodded.

"What's your name?"

"Tavon."

"Okay. You're a freshman too?" she asked, looking at how tall and cute he was with his brown skin, curly hair, and perfect smile, standing over six feet tall.

"No, a junior. I just take the same English class as you."

"I see. Where you from?" Fatima walked into the cafe area full of students who were eating and talking loudly.

"Baltimore."

"Oh shit, me too. What part?"

"I'm from west B-more. How about you?" Tavon could tell from her swag Fatima was from Baltimore or New York.

"Southeast section," she said proudly, loving where she grew up.

"Okay. You on lunch break?"

"Yeah."

"Me too. Let's get a coffee and talk for a second," he requested.

"You sure your girlfriend will like that?" Fatima asked, fishing.

"Sorry, I'm single. How about you?"

"Single as can be," she shot back, getting to know Tavon her whole lunch break.

***

Westside B-more

HD cruised down Eden Street in his Cadillac truck, playing slow jams, about to pick up the young freak he would trick on from time to time when in the mood, which had been every Friday lately. He had met Roseia at a car show two months ago downtown and had been fucking shawty since. HD was an ugly nigga, but he would pay for a bad bitch any day of the week, especially one with a head game like Roseia.

Pulling up in front of her crib, he saw the block was dark and dry tonight, but tomorrow would be the first and shit would be going crazy.

Last night he got a call from X requesting a sit down with him, which seemed odd, but the two men never really crossed paths in the small city. The only thing they had in common was the crazy heated war with Proof and his people. For years, HD hated the Scott family. He tried everything to get rid of Proof, but nothing seemed to work and he had been running outta ideas lately.

Roseia came outside, putting lip gloss on the phat lips everybody loved to death, including HD. Her outfit was a Gucci mini dress with a cute pair of peep-toe heels to go with her fly. Roseia's curves stuck out like a traffic sign. If she wasn't a hoe, she might've made someone a great trophy wife.

"Hi daddy. I missed you," she said, jumping in, giving him a kiss on the cheeks because he didn't do the lip shit unless it was wifey.

"You look cute, shawty." He touched her thighs.

"Thanks, but I'ma look cuter naked," Roseia said, reaching for his zipper to give him a taste before they pulled off. She held his full length and slowly traced her tongue around the tip before going deep, burying her face

"Hmmmm." HD watched her go to work, holding on to the back of her wig.

Roseia saw a shadow from the driver's side window and when she looked up, all she could see was flames from the light.

Boc! Boc! Boc! Boc! Boc! Boc! Boc! Boc!

Roseia caught a head tap and her head fell into HD's lap while he was shot four times. Sunny ran off into the dark night without looking back.

Chapter 8
PG County, Maryland

Proof hated traveling with any drugs or money, but he made an exception today because he had a lot of shit to do after dropping off the duffle bag full of dog food to his brother.

ReRe was holding down the shops today while he took care of business. He loved his wife. She was a real trooper and always stood by his side. There were times she had taken trips for him, moving a car fill of kilos from state to state.

Rags had gone to school so Proof had more than enough time to get his shit together before he got out, but today Rags had basketball practice.

He got in the Tahoe truck with black tints, driving out of his garage, and played some DMX, one of his favorite rappers.

Driving down the street, Proof stopped at a stop sign and fixed the duffle bag in the backseat, placing it under the passenger seat. By the time he lifted himself up, black vans, cars, and SUVs swamped in on him from every side.

Proof wasn't about to go out like no sucker with forty kilos in the truck, so he smashed the gas, running into a Ford truck, knocking it out of his way and racing away. The feds were in a line, chasing him like a madman, trying to keep up. Proof made a left, bending a corner, which was his worst mistake. Not aware of the commercial van backing out of a driveway, Proof slammed right into it, almost losing consciousness if it wasn't for the airbags.

The feds surrounded the truck with guns drawn, snatched him out, and tossed Proof on the floor putting the kingpin in pink cuffs to be funny. The local news pulled up on time to record the top story and breaking news of the day.

***

Downtown B-more

"Jordan, can you please attend to the customer outside who requested a tire change?" ReRe asked her new worker. She was on the phone with a rim company in L.A., ordering a bulk of rims ranging from 18-inch rims to 28-inch rims for all the shops so they could have everything in stock. Summer was about to be near so ReRe knew it was time to order a big shipment, plus business was going so well.

After hanging up, two white men entered, looking around, moving weird, but ReRe continued to play with the computer, typing in the new items' order numbers.

"Excuse me, do you have a size 20-inch rim I can put on an Acura truck?" one of the white men asked.

"Yes. The section over there is for 20 inches, sir," ReRe said, turning around and pointing at the wall.

Before she could turn back around, a SWAT team of federal agents rushed the establishment. ReRe looked like she wanted to run, but the two white guys who she thought were customers had their weapons aimed at her ready.

"Don't try, bitch. You're under arrest for drug trafficking, money laundering, and conspiracy to commit more than one murder" one of the federal agents said like a real robot, putting her in cuffs.

ReRe couldn't believe what was taking place. Everything felt like a movie, but in slow motion. Stepping outside the shop, cameras and lights were everywhere, like she was a big-time famous entertainer going to jail. ReRe tried to breathe but she couldn't, and her vision got blurry. Then her body collapsed. She passed out in the hands of two agents, who called medical assistance.

***

Baltimore Private School

Rags wanted to take a nap in class but his teacher didn't play that. She would make him stay after school and Rags had basketball practice today, so he knew what needed to be done to stay awake.

"Mr. Scott, the principal would like to see you in his office," his teacher, Ms. Rey, said as she got off her walkie-talkie. Every teacher and staff in the school had a walkie-talkie to keep each other informed of any life-threatening events or for communication.

The whole class looked at Rags as if he was in trouble. Rags fixed his uniform and took the walk of shame, which is what the students called walking to the principal office. It wasn't far from Ms. Rey's class.

All types of thoughts ran through his head before knocking on the office door that belonged to Mr. Lejean, an old black army vet who didn't play no games.

"Come inside, Mr. Scott!" Mr. Lejean shouted.

Rags saw two white men in suits and a fat black woman he never saw before in his life.

"I'm Federal Agent Barnes and this is my partner, Agent Springfield. Oh, also, we have a child caseworker, Ms. Toddson. I'ma give it to you raw since you're sixteen years old. Both of your parents have been arrested and won't be back for a very long time. You will be going with Mrs. Toddson until someone can legally look after you. Now, this is between you and I, no one else." Agent Barnes smiled. "do you have any info about your parents selling drugs, committing murders, or any crimes? " Agent Barnes asked with a smirk as he looked at Rags, who had sat unmoved for two minutes.

"Suck my dick and balls," Rags replied, shocking everybody in the room.

"Take him away!" Agent Barnes shouted, ready to fuck Rags.

Mrs. Toddson took Rags to a nearby group home until a loved one could come get him.

Chapter 9
North Baltimore

Days after Rags' parents' arrests, Five and Sunny got Rags outta the group home and moved him into his own apartment, but Five acted as if he was the guardian. Five had other plans for the sixteen-year-old young'un - direct orders from Proof.

Rags laid in his new bed asleep, but he felt someone over him. When he opened his eyes, two handguns were pointed at him.

"Wake your black ass up. Training starts today," Five said, leaning into Rags, shaking his head and laughing because his little nephew was about to become a full man.

"Next time sleep with your gun, dumb muthafucker," Sunny said, standing there and lowering his gun.

"What gun? I don't have one," Rags said, yawning, wiping the crust out of his eyes.

"Here. Now you got two. Don't leave home without it or go to sleep without it." Five grabbed Sunny's gun and tossed it on the bed with his weapon.

"Get yourself ready. We got a long day today," Sunny said, leaving with Five on his trials.

Rags climbed outta bed feeling like he was in boot camp for the streets. Proof had sent word from the Baltimore city correctional center, telling Five to get Rags ready for his new life. Rags had no clue his dad sold drugs, but it all started to make sense how he was able to live like a boss. Never in his dream did he see himself being an up-and-coming drug dealer. Basketball was his only dream. But now he felt it might be slowly fading away overnight. The feds took all of Proof's business establishments and their homes as well as the luxury cars. Rags still didn't fully know what was going on, but he somewhat knew enough to see shit was all bad. Next week would be his dad's and mom's first court date, so he planned to attend, since the jail said he was too young to visit at sixteen years old.

Walking out of his room, he saw Sunny and Five sitting at a table with a kilo of heroin, a scale, fentanyl, cut, masks, gloves, and small baggies to place the tan substance in if he ever choose to bag up work, but the Scott family only sold birds.

"Welcome to Dope 101, cuz. This shit you can never learn in school, yo," Sunny said.

"Today we gonna teach you how to cut heroin, weigh grams and kilos, bag it, and what to cut the shit with correctly, because if you don't use enough, you can kill a gang of people. Then the feds come," Five stated, knowing a few niggas doing twenty years because someone died off dope overdosing.

"We also gonna show you the trick to give fiends the nod. Our dope be the rawest in B-more, and that's why niggas hate us, young nigga. Ya hear me?" Sunny began, showing Rags the ropes as he sat there and soaked up the game.

For a week straight, Sunny and Five did nothing but show Rags the game, from how to cut dope, sell it, shoot a gun, and how to kill. Rags took everything in and he was in love with the lifestyle he never would imagine being a part of.

The next assignment for Rags was to build his own crew of young savages, and he knew the right place to go: Perkin Homes in the southeast section, where he grew up.

Rags put school on hold, changed his number, and focused on his new lifestyle he thought wasn't ready for him.

***

Baltimore City Police Station

Dozen grabbed his coat, ready to meet up with Longhead and Haper, two dirty cops from the station that every drug dealer truly hated. On his way out the door, someone called his name. Captain Flags, his boss, walked up to him, giving Dozen a firm handshake, as always.

Captain Flags had been on the force thirty plus years and became captain his 17th year there. He was a well-respected guy who always got the job done.

"Any new leads on your ex-partner's case?" asked Captain Flags with a look of concern.

"No sir, but I'm on it right now as we speak. Trust and believe, I'ma catch those cocksuckers."

"I'm sure of it. But keep me posted. The mayor and me about to go out for lunch, on him," Captain Flags bragged.

"Oh shit, it must be your fucking birthday! We all know how cheap the mayor is, sir." Dozen hated the mayor. He thought the old fart was a racist bastard.

"The big case all over TV, Proof and his girl, the mayor was very pleased about," Captain Flags said, smiling ear to ear as if he made the arrest.

The feds had teamed up with Captain Flags' department to bring down the city's biggest kingpin since Big Man. Dozen and none of the other detectives or officer knew about this bust. It was private information because the feds believed Proof had inside help with every police station in Maryland. Nobody had a clue that Dozen was a part of the Scott family or Proof's brother because years before becoming a cop, he changed his last name to Fields, the last name of his lovely wife.

"You're on your way to chief of police, I'm telling you." Dozen boosted his boss's ego outta this world.

"I know. I can feel it."

"You deserve it, boss Nobody works as hard as you, not even *The First 48*," Dozen said, sharing a laugh with his boss.

"I always knew there was a reason why I liked my head detective." Captain Flags patted Dozen on his back before walking off with his head high into the sky.

"Fucking clown," Dozen mumbled, walking out of the building for his meeting with his two crime buddies to plot a new drug bust amongst the three of them. But nobody would call it in and all the funds will be split down the middle. This is why Dozen loved being a cop.

Chapter 10
Downtown B-more
Months later

Rags' name quickly spread through the city as he became an overnight star in the murder capital. Ever since his uncle and brother Sunny showed him the game, he masterminded a big drug ring running through Maryland down to D.C. In a matter of months, Rags was starting to see Jay-Z money at sixteen years old. Rags had two condos, four luxury cars, and every designer brand he could think of or find. His crew had different areas of the city on lock from the eastside to the Westside, but his stomping grounds were of course southeast Baltimore.

The opening door of his condo startled him and he reached for the Glock 40 laying on the expensive glass table.

"Chill, yo, it's only me, scared nigga. What you all jumpy for, shawty?" Bigs said. He was a close friend Rags grew up with from Lincoln Hill, but he had moved to southeast.

"Nigga, it's a cold game. I'm always on point, bro." Rags put the gun down, looking at the book bag in Bigs' hand.

"This the 170,000 from Bank Street on the Southside." Bigs tossed him the bag, going to the kitchen for a bottle of water.

"Yo holla at ya?" Rags asked, using his city B-more slang. They called everybody Yo or Shawty. It was a B-more thing since way back.

"Who, Kanno?"

"No, nigga, he stopped this morning. I'm taking 'bout Volume." Rags needed to speak with Volume because his little brother went to VA with twenty kilos of Rags' and nobody ever heard from him again.

"Dude may be hiding out too because nobody saw him," Bigs said.

"A'ight, shawty we gonna focus on this load coming in tonight. This going to set us all the way straight, yo."

"I already spoke to my brother and cousins out in D.C., so they ready" Bigs had family in D.C. working for him moving close to thirty birds a week - on a good day, of course.

"They some wild niggas, but they got money, no doubt." Rags saw the wind from outside push his front door a little.

"I forgot to close the door. My bad, yo." Bigs always did this and it pissed Rags off.

"What if we had drugs in this bitch, bro? Come on, use your fat-ass head!" Rags yelled on him.

"Nigga, you not dumb enough to shit where you rest," Bigs added, turning on the living room TV just as the door got kicked in off the frame.

Rags and Bigs both reached for the gun on the glass table, thinking it was ops busting in on them.

"FBI! Get on the ground now!"

A crew of federal agents rushed the crib, arresting both men, taking them to a low-key warehouse the feds used as a hold over.

***

"Young Scott, you had a short run, but as far as we can tell, it was a damn good one," Agent Clossal said, looking over his shoulder to Agent Carter.

"A run that's gonna get you forty-five years, if you lucky," Agent Carter added, playing tag team.

"We got a lot of shit on you and your crew, Rags: wire taps and murders, all leading back to you." Agent Clossal pointed at Rags, seeing he was unmoved by the whole conversation.

"Guess who our star witnesses are, playboy? Because from the looks of it, you think we joking, huh, bitch?" Agent Carter grabbed a folder from a table behind him and opened it directly in front of Rags, who sat quiet, knowing the game his family taught him months ago.

"Volume and his little brother Geezy both wrote statements and said they're willing to go all the way to trial to get you off the streets. Geezy said you made him drive to VA with twenty kilos and unfortunately, he got pulled over and gave you up," Agent Clossal explained, shaking his head.

"You young and handsome with a whole life ahead of you. Help me get you back on the streets." Agent Carter's voice softened.

"We don't want you, Rags. Give us whoever is selling you the keys. We need your plug and all this will go away. Them dudes in the federal jails like Big Sandy, Hazelton, and Beaumont USP are raping youngstas like you, taking your manhood, leaving you with nothing," said Agent Clossal.

"Unless you want your manhood snatched," Agent Carter replied, seeing his partner almost bust out in laughter.

"Look at your mom and dad. Their lives are done. Do you wanna follow their path? I know you smart because you almost beat us, but nobody can outsmart the feds," Agent Clossal stated, hoping Rags gave in because his friend Bigs didn't say a word the whole time they played good cop/bad cop on him.

"Okay." Rags spoke his first word as the agents gave each other a dap, ready to do their insiders-only dance.

"Take your time. We gonna protect you, and if you wanna sell drugs, we will supply you so your team can flood the whole city. Then once you done locking up a few hoods, we can send you to another state. We do it all the time. So tell us, who supplies you?" Agent Carter asked as the room got quiet.

"Santa," Rags said

"Who the fuck is——" Agent Clossal was about ready to slap the black off his face.

"You picked the wrong ones. I'ma make sure they bury your ass just like your fucking no-good father, you hear me?" Agent Carter almost lost his cool as other agents came inside to grab ahold of their co-worker, who had a long résumé of beating up drug dealers.

"Your game, kid. We tried to give you a way out, but you taking the hard route, kiddo." Agent Clossal stood up to leave, hoping to change Rags' mind with a quick one-on-one session.

"Fuck you, pig. Call my lawyer!" Rags shot back.

"You don't get a call. You underage and we found seven handguns in your room during a search. One of them got a dead body on it of a young white girl who was recently killed at a bus stop on her way to school when a drive-by took place. Looks like we found our shooter." The agent smiled, leaving the room.

Rags never had seven guns or did a drive-by, so he knew the feds were playing dirty with him. All types of thoughts were running through Rags' head, like how much time he was facing, if Bigs remained silent, why Volume and Geezy snitched, who else the feds picked up, and a lawyer Five had on retainer for him. Rags' young life was moving before his eyes.

Chapter 11
Baltimore Detention City, Maryland
Months later

Rags sat in the prison dayroom playing a card game called casino with his co-defendant Bigs. This is where some federal inmates came to fight their cases, but Rags and Bigs were both young, so they were jailed on the minor side of the jail.

Last week Rags and Bigs, thanks to Five, paid a lawyer, who showed up with all smiles. The lawyer told them the DA was willing to drop the murder charge if they both copped out to five years in federal prison.

Both men knew the murder weapon the feds ended up charging both of them with was bogus and a lie because they refused to snitch. At first Rags thought his whole crew was being indicted, but it was only him and Bigs. The feds only had Rags on wiretap telling Geezy to "score that 20-yard touch in VA" on a certain day. Geezy explained to the feds that twenty yards was short for twenty kilos. Bigs had a bullshit sale to a federal informer, which turned out to be Volume, the brother of Geezy.

Rags knew the feds wanted him to rat on his dad, uncle, and brother, but Rags was sticking to the code of the streets. When they got the recent offer, Rags and Bigs weren't too happy because the feds didn't have anything really on them, but seeing how they was giving other niggas in their unit twenty years and life sentences, they had been considering it.

An old Muslim cat who worked the law library looked at Rags' case to help him because he had known Five for years. He explained to Rags how the feds didn't play fair and how they could arrest people off word of mouth. He also pointed out the wiretap they had on him was enough to send him away for five to ten years.

"You always cheating," Rags said, slamming the cards on the table because Bigs kept adding up wrong numbers and quickly snatching the cards.

"What you mean?' Bigs smirked.

"Nigga, five plus two is seven, dumbass, not nine."

"My bad, yo. Everybody ain't go to a private school," Bigs added.

"You ain't go to school period."

"Well, as long as I can count money, I'm good, shawty." Bigs laughed

"You can't even do that shit right, my nigga."

"What you think about what the white Jewish man said?" Bigs asked in a low voice because niggas were nosy in the day room all day eavesdropping.

"Who, the lawyer?"

"Yeah, dumb-dumb."

"To be real, outta five, all we do is 3 or 4 years with good behavior. It's non-violent so we can even take programs."

"You think so?" Bigs was in deep thought and now it wasn't sounding too bad.

"I won't do it unless you do it, yo," Rags said to his friend, who was still soul searching.

"A'ight. Let's take it and come home shining." Bigs smiled

Rags heard an inmate yell the C.O., who said he had a visit, so he jetted for the shower because earlier Rags had done five hundred push-ups. While in the shower, he wondered who it was because Five and Sunny sent messages through the lawyer. Proof and ReRe were still fighting their cases and his boys were all getting money still, but laying low. His boys Kanno and Fat P wrote letters daily and sent money, but visits to a fed jail was a big NO.

***

The visitation room was packed with people's loved ones so it made Rags look harder to see if he recognized anyone there. In the right corner he saw the most beautiful young woman in there waving at him. Rags couldn't believe who had come to see him. His heart raced a hundred miles per hour as the palm of his hands got moist.

"Hi Carena."

“Should I call you Doug or Rags?” She gave him a disappointed look.

When Rags got locked up, he didn’t have any way to connect Carena because the feds had his cell phone and shut down all the social media pages he had up.

“I guess you heard what happened?” he said, putting his head down.

“The whole school did, right before I graduated, Doug. I was calling you for weeks, stalking your IG page and Facebook, praying the rumors wasn’t true.” She got emotional because she really missed him and liked Rags a lot. He had always been different and stood out.

“I’m sorry, Carena, but it’s in my bloodline. The streets chose my soul. This is me and who I’ve become”

“Doug, you’re sixteen. You don’t know what you’re meant to be. Why cut yourself short?”

“You will never understand.”

“No, you’re wrong, I do, but just because your mom and dad in the feds for selling drugs doesn’t mean you have to learn from this,” she explained as she saw him getting upset.

“Carena, you don’t know shit about my parents or life. You came from a spoon-fed household.” He hurt her feelings.

“Oh, it’s like that? You know what? I’m here to show support as your girl no matter what. I’m in college down south trying to make a good life for me and you if you’re willing to leave this life alone when your released”

“Carena, I don’t need nobody. I’m a young boss and this is my life now. Take it or kick rocks,”

“Wow, Doug, really?” She was shocked.

“Yeah, but better yet, I’ll do you the solid.” Rags stood up and walked off the floor, leaving her crying in front of everybody.

Chapter 12
Big Sandy USP, KY
Present time

Rags couldn't sleep all night as he tossed and turned, thinking about his big day release day tomorrow. When he copped out to his five years a few years back, he never knew the time would fly as it did. Luckily Rags only had to do three years and some months in total. Bigs was in another prison in PA behind the wall fucking his bid up, stabbing dudes and smoking K-2 fake. His brother and uncle told him they would be waiting outside the gate for him tomorrow.

Every day he thought about how easy it could have been if only he would have snitched, but that wasn't in the Scott family blood.

Last year, his dad and mom took the feds to trial and both blew. Proof received a life sentence plus forty-five years and ReRe got sentenced to thirty-seven years on her prison term.

Rags kept in touch with his parents through Corrlinks email. His dad was in Victorville USP in Cali and ReRe was being held at a women's jail in West Virginia. The time they took for standing tall said a lot to Rags. He would forever live on their legacy and family name. While in prison, Rags took up some real estate classes and got his licenses, so now he planned to buy homes and flip them in the urban neighborhoods. Selling drugs was the first thing on his to-do list. Most niggas came to jail and talked all that how they were gonna get back out and make a difference, but a lot of them lied. Rags heard it all before. Rags' team, Kanno and Fat P, were both getting big money in the city with Sunny, but everybody knew once Rags touched he'd be supplying. He also heard about a few new big-time dealers in the city, Polo and LB. There was another nigga named Sean P who worked for HD locking shit down, but the war going on fucked up a lot of money, from what he had been hearing.

He checked the time. It read 3:47 a.m. He had two and a half more hours before the doors popped open. Rags only told two of his close boys he was going home because niggas be hating. Last month Rags saw a prisoner toss a knife in a nigga's cell and drop a slip telling the police about the knife he saw in cell 201. The police sent

Ra, who had a day until he went home to the box, for the knife someone planted on him. After 15 years in prison, Ra had to stay 41 extra days in the box because of a hater.

When Rags' eyelids shut, he took a nap, thankful for where his life was at and heading. But there were still a few who had to feel his wrath from their betrayal.

***

The early morning couldn't have come any quicker. Rags was escorted out of the prison gates with a debit card full of the money he had on his commissary account.

Sunny and Five both were leaning on an all-white clean Mercedes-Benz Maybach that had new car tags. The front license plate read RAGS in bold letters.

"Nah, shawty, y'all did it big." Rags smiled upon seeing the fly-ass car.

"Anything for you, nephew," Five said, giving him a bear hug.

"You deserve it, shawty. You stood tall, holding the family name down," Sunny said, embracing him with a duffle bag full of money.

"Goddamn, I feel like Big Meech out in dis bitch." Rags laughed, peeping into the duffle bag to see crispy blue face hundreds in rubber band stacks. Even though Rags had a lot of money saved up, it wouldn't hurt to add some more to his collection.

"Let's put some highway miles on this new car of yours. Shit, I don't even got a Maybach," Sunny stated.

"Who bought this for me?"

"Your dad and mom. They always spoke about getting you a Maybach when you turned 18, but due to your situation, you got it at twenty years old. I had my people make you a license at the local DMV so you can drive," Five stated, driving away from the prison.

"Thanks, yo."

"We got you an apartment and a wardrobe, Chanel to Dior, little shawty. I know how you do," Sunny said, laughing because

Rags had the most swag in the family beside their father. He was the king of drip.

"I'm ready to hop back in dem streets," Rags boasted.

"You know, Rags, you older now. Open a business. Why risk your life if you don't have to? Me and Sunny do this because it's what we become. You still got a future ahead of yourself. Do that real estate shit and be legit," Five said, driving while looking in the rearview mirror here and there, praying Rags took heed to his words.

"I already made up my mind I'ma live and die in the streets." Rags' words were firm. He saw Five and Sunny look at each other with a saddened look, but they knew the young'un's blood type was solid hustle.

"Since you back, let me update you," Sunny broke the silence.

"That's what I'm talking about." Rags played with a few buttons in the back, looking for the arm rest, but there were so many buttons and luxury shit he became confused.

"Kanno and Fat P built a strong crew since the day you went in. Southeast is yours, but Kanno moved into an area located on the eastside, and this started a war with some young knucklehead named Polo," Sunny explained, giving Rags the rundown.

"I heard of him."

"Yeah, shawty a getting money nigga who runs with killers. But he's the least of our problems right now," Five stated, slowing down the car, passing state troopers.

"What other issues?" Rags had been hearing a lot of stories about the city and now everything was coming to light.

"You heard of X?" asked Sunny

"I hear he some cold-blooded killer moving birds." Rags saw Five laugh at the comment he made.

"Selling birds, yeah, and killer if pushed. Shawty should be in one of those mosques with them brothers reading a book." Five showed his hate for X.

"Dude very smart. Daddy been at war with him for some time now and that shit don't stop because Daddy's locked up, so we need to get him out the way. To make our problems worse, a nigga named

Sean P is trying to take over my section in the west with the help of his plug and cousin, HD." Sunny shook his head.

"They really from D.C., if you ask me," Five added, telling the truth.

"We build a bigger army, flood more blocks, and kill more opps," Rags said with ease.

"Sounds easy. If that's what you wanna do, we down," Sunny said.

"All in," Five added, knowing the city would turn into a big graveyard in no time.

Chapter 13
Club Mirage, B-more

The packed club called Mirage on 401 West Street had a line around the corner to get inside tonight. Everybody came out dripping in designer gear, rocking their best jewelry to show off, and of course, to attract the city's baddest women.

Rags and his crew were already in the VIP booth popping big bottles of Henny, Casa, Migou, and D'ussé, surrounded by beautiful ladies and gangstas, ready to blow off any second.

"Welcome home, my nigga," Kanno said, putting a glass in the air as everybody followed the crew. Kanno rocked long braids to the side that most in the city called gangstas. He also sported platinum teeth and a big chain.

"Shit about to be different now," Rags told Kanno and Fat P, who wasn't fat no more. He had his weight up, 6'2" and two hundred forty pounds of muscle.

"The streets missed you, bro," Fat P said with his deep voice over the loud Shy Glizzy music playing in the background.

"I know. But tomorrow, meet at my new spot so we can talk. I got some plans," Rags said, watching more pretty women fill the VIP area.

Rags was too busy drinking to peep the crew posted up on the wall next to the exit signs in the far back.

***

Across the club

Polo nodded his head to the beat, sipping on cranberry juice because he didn't drink or smoke. To him, drugging was a sign of weakness and failure.

The past couple of years, Polo and his big brother LB had been making a name for themselves in the drug game, mainly in east B-more, where he was from. Since he was a teen, Polo always wanted more for his mom, who took care of four kids alone because his father got killed in a crack house when they were all young. LB was the oldest, but he spent most of his time behind bars fighting murder cases, and twice he beat and assault charges. Everybody from east B-more knew LB and his murderous crew, who had a long record of killing anybody not from their turf.

"That must be the little nigga everybody been talking about?" Polo asked his best friend Sha.

"Yeah, that's Sunny little brother," Sha said, hating Sunny with a passion because five years ago, Sunny's crew killed Sha older brother and left his body hanging out of a 12-story building.

Sha's older brother Nook was a robber who would rob his own mother if the price was right. Nook ended up robbing one of Sunny's spots and someone saw the 6'6" giant coming out with a Christmas bag full of money and drugs. When word got back to Sunny, he had to do something, so he made a chick line Nook up in his own hood. Sunny's crew tortured Nook in the apartment before hanging his naked body out the window for the world to see.

LB and Nook were best friends, so when he heard about the news while he was in his cell fighting two murders, he wanted blood from Sunny's crew, who had the city on lock with fifteen young bloods.

"I want all them little niggas dead before the end of summer," Polo told Sha and his two other goons, watching the scene on the wall, strapped up.

"Should we air it out now?" one of Polo's shooters asked, already reaching for the moment.

"Nah, shawty, they gonna have their time." Polo put back on his Cartier frames and exited the club, going back to the hood so he could speak to LB, his organization's muscle.

***

North Village, B-more

Rags woke up in his apartment with a mean hangover as the knocking at his front door woke him up. Looking over at the clock on the dresser, he saw that it read 11:35 a.m.

"Damn, yo." He climbed outta bed to someone still banging on his door. He lived in a nice area surrounded by white people with good-paying jobs, so he didn't need no unwanted attention to him or the new spot.

Rags made it to the front door and snatched it open to see Kanno and Fat P laughing and talking loudly.

"Yo, y'all niggas know I do live in a white neighborhood."

"So?" Fat P shrugged his shoulders

"That means white people call police, asshole," Rags said, walking in the kitchen to find something to eat, but he hadn't even had a chance to go food shopping.

"Get your panties out your ass, little nigga. You ain't get no pussy last night?" Kanno asked.

"Hell nah he didn't, look at him," Fat P joked.

"Pussy the last thing on my mind," Rags lied. He wanted some badly, but he wasn't about to just fuck anything that would kill his clout.

"Remy asked about you last night," Kanno stated.

"Who that?" Rags remembered the name, but couldn't match the face.

"She lived a few doors down from you in Perkin Homes, shawty," Fat P added.

"The dark-skinned bad little bitch who always had a fatty," Kanno said. He always wanted to smash Remy, but she was stuck up, acting like she didn't fuck with niggas in the hood.

"Oh, ole gurl with the chinky eyes." Rags remembered now. Remy was cool people. They used to play ball with her brother Punch.

"Shawty a nurse now," Fat P said, on his phone texting a stripper bitch, who had been stalking him to pay for her abortion.

"What happened to Punch? He used to play ball with us and yo was nice," Rags stated.

"Sean P and them niggas slumped shawty when we was warring with them niggas." Kanno's voice was sad.

"Now that you mention them niggas and we all here, shit about to level up out here," Rags said.

"What you mean? Shit going good, bro," Fat P said.

"No, it's not, I got the rundown. Niggas trying to take over our shit, and we have to show theses niggas who runs the city. I got my brother's crew and Five's crew backing us, so now I want to build a bigger army"

"So you want to recruit niggas?" Kanno asked, knowing niggas don't work for free and they had been having a hard time feeding their own soldiers.

"Yes."

"But we only getting fifteen to seventeen kilos a week, if that."

"Don't worry. Shit about to change. We about to have the ops' soldiers coming to work for us once we take over their blocks," Rags said.

His boys were all in, ready to see Rags' plan come to light because he was a young mastermind.

Chapter 14
Westside B-more

Dozen, Haper, and Longhead watched the boarded-up house from a block down on a late Friday night. Most people new to these slums would assume the building was shut down, but all the dope fiend in the area knew otherwise.

"How much you think they bringing in?" Dozen asked Haper from the driver's seat, watching people walk in and out a small alleyway leading into the back.

"Tonight we shall find out," Dozen replied

"I call nights like this Good Friday." Longhead cracked an evil grin.

All three men were the city's most hated dirty cops who would extort a baby if he had the right amount of money. They planted drugs on niggas, robbed dealers, shot innocent people, sold drugs to other dealers, and sometimes they would rob a dealer then turn back and resell him the work.

"I think we got the best job in the world," Haper said.

"You think?" Longhead added.

"We street cops who do as we please. Who the fuck is above us, the law?" Dozen asked.

"He's fucking right." Longhead saw a silver BMW truck pull up.

"That's our guy," Haper said as a young man climbed out of the driver's seat with a brown paper bag and a Gucci book bag.

"I believe so. Crunch time," said Dozen, pulling down his mask.

***

Blaze carried the two empty bags into the back alley on his way into the back door, where Jus was waiting for him to collect the weekly funds so he could bring it to his cousin Sean P. Working for someone like Sean P, they had to always make sure the funds were all intact or that could cause a problem, because one thing Sean P didn't play about was money and his jewelry. Blaze had built a name for himself in the streets, mainly on the west, because he didn't fuck with the east.

"Right on time," Lil Yay said, pushing a begging fiend to the side so Blaze could get in.

"How y'all little niggas looking out here, shawty?" Blaze asked, walking inside the dim, abandoned building, looking at piles of bundles stacked up on the wall ready to be dished out.

"We got the money," Caleo said, going to grab a knapsack full of paper as two young shooters eyed the boss man.

"Y'all little niggas need to be in school somewhere, not in the trap." Blaze remembered when he was young and school was all he knew.

"Man, fuck school," one of them stated, laughing, puffing on a blunt.

"How old are you, yo?" Blaze looked at them both, but really was talking to the big head kid.

"Sixteen."

"If I come back and ever see you in this trap again, I'ma whip your—"

"My mom be here," the kid shot back.

"She smokes?"

"I sell her all her shit. Better me than making someone else pockets phatter." The kid shrugged to his own comment.

Blaze knew he made sense, but Blaze still didn't like the fact of kids selling drugs.

Caleo stepped out of the darkness with a bag of money, handing it to Blaze, who emptied everything on the floor about to count it all. Last time Caleo shorted him 20,000, but Blaze replaced it with his own and didn't mention a word. But if it happened today, Blaze made plans to kill him.

"Damn, bro, you know you can trust me," Caleo said with a nervous look.

"I don't trust a soul, not even my own." Blaze continued to count the money before hearing gunshots.

Three masked men rushed the crib. Caleo and his young boys reached for their weapons, but it was a fatal mistake.

Bloc! Bloc! Bloc! Bloc! Bloc!

The crew laid everybody down in the abandoned building except Blaze, who stood there looking dumbfounded with no gun on him. Blaze kept a gun in the trunk of his SUV, but he felt like if he ever needed, he could box a nigga.

"Don't look so worried now." Dozen spoke first, taking off his mask.

"Oh fuck." Blaze knew who Dozen was the moment the mask came off. Now he knew it would turn out bad regardless.

"It's me, the boogeyman," Dozen joked while his crew bagged up the money and dug into the dead victims' pockets.

"Just let me live, yo. You can have all that shit."

"I know, I took it, didn't I?" Dozen said before pulling the trigger.

"Call it in and let them know the robbery suspect got away on foot. I'ma go run down the block and fire off some shots. Longhead, take the money to the car," Haper said, running outside as everybody stuck to the plan.

Dozen called it in on the walkie-talkie.

***

Downtown B-more

Carena drove a new E-class Mercedes-Benz to her business lunch meeting with the head DA, which was her aunty, for the federal system of Maryland. Carena had recently finished college last month and already was hired by one of the top firms in the city and she was more than proud of herself. Life for the beautiful young lady seemed to be all about work. Last night she got her first caseload so she had been at her office downtown focused on it. The DA's system was all about making a name for yourself and cracking the biggest cases for a verdict. Luckily, her aunty had been schooling Carena, trying to show the young lady the ropes.

Carena heard from a high school friend that Rags was recently released from prison and looking good. She tried to act like she didn't give two damns but in reality, Carena couldn't help but to think about him. She hated Rags for leaving her that day she came to visit him. But she couldn't be involved with a criminal. Carena wanted to tell Rags she was going to school to become a DA, but the whole thing was bad timing to her. Now that he was home, Carena planned to stay far away to protect her heart.

Chapter 15
Westside, B-more

The sun was out and the weather had people coming outside with barely nothing on. It was days like this Sean P loved to come out and give back to the hood with his crew. In the summer, Sean P would throw block parties, basketball events, kid events, and big-time giveaways. He was from D.C., but the streets of B-more raised him. Sean P grew very adapted to the street life, seeing his uncle HD flood the heroin capital with more keys than he could ever imagine.

Once HD put him on to his first kilo, Sean P ain't look back. He built a crew of hustlers and killers. Sean P knew every hustler wasn't a killer and vice versa, so he always separated the two fields.

The big issue going on was Five and Sunny. They were a pain in his ass for years now. He tried to have them killed so many times, but it was like the Scott family had nine lives. Now he recently heard their little nephew got out of the feds, but Sean P wasn't worried about a little nigga. He had bigger problems. Yesterday someone killed his cousin and robbed his spot, leaving nothing inside except dead bodies. He had a clue who could have done it. His money was on Five's people. Sean P's motorcycle zoomed down the street to meet his workers Volume and Geezy, two of his most loyal soldiers. The brothers had been doing a rack of killing for Sean P and HD lately, so he wanted to know if they knew anything or had heard any info yet.

A group of young niggas filled the block, surrounding Volume and Geezy telling war stories and laughing until the black motorcycle pulled up turning off its engine. Volume and Geezy both made their way over to their boss who, didn't look so happy.

"What's going on, shawty? You don't come around these parts much," Volume said, knowing something didn't seem right.

"Something happened to Caleo and Blaze." Sean P's voice was low and sad.

"Blaze?" Geezy said, in shock, because for a nigga to play with Blaze, they must have had a death wish.

"Yeah. They ran in the spot on Washington and took everything, yo." Sean P still couldn't believe the disrespect.

"Yo, I think niggas said something about that shit earlier," Volume said, thinking back, trying to remember who brought it up. Volume had no idea it was his people who been killed.

"Did they say who did it?" Sean P asked tensely.

"Nah, but I'ma find out."

"Me too, bro. Shit about go up now," Geezy said, patting his weapon.

"That's what I like to hear. I'ma go get up with ole head. Call me with any new details," Sean P stated, peeling off with murder on his mind.

***

Victorville USP, Cali

Proof had been on the Westside in a dangerous maximum-security prison, locked away for years, but he was financially at peace. Getting sentenced to life plus forty-five years made him feel hopeless, but at the same time, he knew what it was before signing up for the street shit. He lived with no regret whatsoever. If he could do it over, he would in a second. With his family in position, he could sleep at night. When ReRe got arrested with him, Proof did everything in his power to get her released beside rat, but the feds wanted to prove a point. Five paid for their appeal lawyer, who put in a direct appeal, but got shot down off the rip. Now the lawyer was working on a 2255 motion to get them out of jail.

Proof had been going down to Jummah and getting back on his Muslim deen because he was a born Muslim, but rarely practiced until now. He started studying and doing a lot of Islamic reading. The unit was always loud, but he spent most of his time in the cell reading and writing short stories. Proof ran into a few dudes who wrote books and he wanted to get into that lane. With Rags being home, he felt better knowing his son was outta the system, but he prayed the life that got him in prison won't be his downfall. He was very proud of his daughter Fatima, who became a Baltimore City cop this year. Proof wanted his baby girl to stay focused and out of the way of people like Dozen, her uncle. At first when Fatima told him she wanted to become a cop, he frowned upon it, but then realized Fatima was a civilian and not a street person. She didn't have to live by the code of the streets because she wasn't in them unlike him.

In two more years, if he stayed outta trouble, his counselor promised he would be shipped to a FC/prison close to New York.

***

Downtown Baltimore

Fatima loved her blue police uniform. She rocked it with pride and strength. Becoming a cop felt so good to her because now she could help people.

Since graduating college, her life had been close to perfect. She had a nice condo, nice car, on and off boyfriend, and overall, she was very happy and grateful. Her uncle worked at the same police station, but she never saw him, nor did she mention his name.

The other day she heard someone saying how much of a dirt bag Dozen was and Fatima acted like she didn't even care because she didn't. Nobody knew this, but when Fatima was a kid, she spent the night over at his house and Dozen touched her in places no man should at the young age of seven. Fatima never felt the same since Every time he would come around, Fatima would rush the opposite way to avoid the anger. She didn't tell anybody because she felt like nobody would believe her, so Fatima kept it to herself and hadn't spoken a word to him since.

She rushed to the locker room to punch in to start her early 6 a.m. shift, which was perfect because at 3 p.m. when she normally got off, Fatima would hit the gym with her personal trainer from New York named Romell, who worked her good every time.

Fatima's body was curvy, toned, and perfect, thanks to dieting plus training. Health was one of her main focuses.

Chapter 16
Little Italy, Baltimore

Volume and Geezy sat in their mother's living room, waiting on Sunday dinner to be done. The brothers came here every Sunday for their mom's big meals she always made after church.

"I can't believe niggas took out Blaze. Dude was good people. I liked shawty. He didn't play 'bout that paper," Geezy stated, sitting on the couch shaking his head.

"Yeah, I bet it was Kanno's bitch ass," Volume added, having a strong dislike for all southeast niggas, even though they were from there.

"Maybe it was Five."

"Yo, speaking of them niggas, I heard through a bitch I'm fucking that she saw Rags in a club like two weeks ago," Volume said as Geezy looked worried.

"Southeast Rags?" Geezy hoped not because if word got out that he and Volume snitched on him their street stripes would be gone.

"Yeah, big money Rags." Volume smirked

"This is bad, bro. What the fuck we gonna do?" Geezy quickly panicked.

"Relax, yo, we good. If bro knew it was us, he would have been sent word to the streets." Volume had thought about Rags coming home for years.

"You think so?"

"Facts. The police told us we was good any way" Volume said as if it was nothing

"I don't trust them police."

"You trusted them enough to give up information."

"So did you," Geezy added because Volume told just like he did, but Geezy felt like he had no choice.

"Fuck all them niggas. We run with Sean P now. Them niggas know better to come this way" Volume lifted his shirt, showing his Glock 19.

"Don't let Mama see that." Geezy finished his sentence on cue as his mom came out from the kitchen with two plates full of soul food.

"Don't let me see what?" She paused, looking at her boys, knowing they were up to no good.

"Nothing." Volume smiled.

"Come sit at the table to eat." Their mom still treated them like babies.

"Mama, we grown now," Geezy said, going to the table.

"In your head. Now sit your black ass down," she responded. "Let's say our prayer"

While praying, all three of them had their eyes closed, holding hands, so they were unaware of the two men who snuck in from the back door.

"It's too late to pray now," Rags said, holding a Tommy gun with two hands.

"Oh Lord, help my soul." The elderly lady grabbed her chest looking at her two sons then back to the gunmen.

Volume and Geezy both were shocked and speechless at the sight. Geezy always had nightmares that one day this would catch up to him.

"I - I - I got love for you, big bro. You showed us the game," Geezy fumbled over his words, trying to buy time while plotting an escape.

"So the thanks I get is you ratting on me?" Rags laughed, not peeping Volume slowly sliding his left hand off the table towards his lap.

Bloc!

Bloc!

Bloc!

Rags didn't see Volume reaching, but Kanno did, and he lit his ass up out of the chair with his handgun, a .44 Mag he called Bull-dog.

"My baby! Nooooo!" Volume's mom cried, looking down at the ground while Volume bled out of his mouth.

"Please don't kill me! Take my mom instead." Geezy pointed to his mother, who looked at him confused and uptight.

"You dirty little bastard! I knew I should have swallowed your ungrateful ass," Geezy's mom cursed, something he never heard.

"Mom, I got my whole life ahead of me, and look at you. Mom, sorry, but your life is ruined, over. You can barely walk" Geezy said before his mother reached over the table to slap fire out of his face.

"You're a fucking rat just like your father was. I hope they put a bullet in your skull," she spat.

"You around here acting like the Holy Ghost when you still sneak smoking crack," Geezy said, watching the surprised look on her face.

Kanno and Rags couldn't believe what they were witnessing and they tried their best to hold their laughter in, but it was too funny.

"So what? I was smoking crack when I had your dusty ass and to be honest, I was selling pussy too, so your papa can be anybody, dirt bag." She was on fire

"Damn," Kanno said in disbelief.

"So you lied to us." Geezy was heartbroken because the man who he thought was his dad died in jail.

"Fuck you, bitch! Burn in hell," Geezy's mom said, spitting on her son's face.

"I like this old bitch. They don't make them like her no more," Rags told Kanno.

"Dude tripping." Kanno looked at Geezy before aiming his gun at his head, firing twice, then Rags finished the job and killed the elderly woman.

"Damn, bro, what a day. I'ma remember this shit." Rags laughed on the way out, wishing he could have recorded the whole scene besides the killing.

Chapter 16
West Virginia

In a small place called Bruceton Mills lay Hazelton prison for women. The compound was large with a male side blocked in by fences and walls. ReRe sat down in the yard, letting life soak in, something she tried to do once a day if the jail wasn't on lockdown. A lot of women in the jail had a long time to do just like ReRe, but they turned to violence to relieve stress. Once a month at least, an inmate or correctional guard was being stabbed to death. Staying to herself was what she was best at along with minding her own business because being so far away from home, ReRe was very anti-social. The 35 years she got slapped with was for nothing. The only thing they had ReRe on was placing dirty money into legit-owned businesses. To be given 35 years for no real crime turned her life and outlook on life upside down. Hearing Rags was home made her happy, but when Proof told her Rags still had the street life in his blood, she feared the worst. The system hadn't reformed him. Instead, it had set him up to fail. Since being in jail for the first time, she realized there was no way out the system if you're living a life of crime. The best thing to do is to get out. This was something she explained daily to young women planning to go home and sell pussy or sell drugs with their boyfriends.

ReRe went to walk the track one more time, then prepared to head back to her dorm for dinner.

***

Little Italy, B-more

Fatima arrived at a crime scene in the nice neighborhood in Little Italy, seeing her fellow officers place yellow tape around a house as she hopped out.

"What happened?" she asked a tall white masculine cop.

"Go inside," he shot back with a smile, knowing she was a rookie.

Fatima paid the rude cop no mind as she walked inside the house slowly, seeing people in lab coats taking pictures and dusting off areas for fingerprints. Stepping into the kitchen, she saw blood everywhere and dead bodies, which made her vomit all over the wall.

"Somebody get her the fuck outta here!" a captain yelled, hoping she didn't fuck up evidence. Outside, the same stocky white cop who told her to go inside was laughing upon seeing the vomit juice on her work shirt.

"You'll get them next time, rookie." The cop patted Fatima on her shoulder, walking away, dying in laughter.

Fatima couldn't believe the sight she just witnessed. Whoever killed that family had to be cold-hearted, she thought to herself.

***

Downtown, B-more

HD co-owned a small car lot he let a white friend named Jack run. They had been business partners for years. Last night HD got a call from X requesting a one-on-one sit down. HD never had words with X, but they did have a lot of mutual friends like Jack, who knew X before him, so HD didn't mind sitting down to listen. One thing he did know was they both had a strong hatred for the Scott family. Sean P told him about what happened to Blaze and Caleo and in his mind, that crime scene had Five's or Sunny's name written all over it.

Not too long ago before eating lunch, HD got another call concerning the death of Volume and Geezy, which shocked him because the two little niggas had been putting in a lot of work for him and Sean P. Taking three to four losses back to back would hurt his profits, so HD was already thinking of a get back for the Scott family.

"Harry, your guest is here. I'ma go across town to order some parts for the new Hummer," Jack said, entering HD's small office, calling him by his government.

"A'ight, don't take long, slim, because I gotta go soon," HD said, seeing X approaching the room in a nice suit with glasses and a clean cut.

HD heard X was down with the Nation Of Islam but at first, he didn't believe it, until now.

"Peace, brother," X stated, sitting down across from HD.

"Pleased to meet you."

"Same to you. We have a lot of connections out here and I think it was due time for this," X spoke strong and clear.

"I agree, brother. So what brings you here? I'm sure you don't want to buy a car, seeing that Bentley SUV you arrived in."

"The Scott family," was all X needed to say to catch HD's attention as he sat up straight.

"Yes, they're becoming a pain in my ass," HD admitted.

"I heard about your losses. I'm sure that was due to them, I suppose?" X looked him in his eyes, seeing HD was a little embarrassed.

HD was a man of pride and honor. He never wanted or needed help with anything at all.

"They got lucky."

"I'm here to make sure them fools don't get lucky again," X said.

"You have a plan?"

"Something like that. But I'ma need your help on this."

"I'm down 100%." HD smiled.

"Is that right?"

"Yeah. Whatever needs to be done, we will do it. Have no worries," HD explained

"Good. Let's start with this weekend."

"I'm listening," HD said, paying close attention.

Chapter 17
Virginia Beach, VA

Sunny took his girlfriend Rachel out to Virginia Beach for her birthday weekend. He wanted to get away from the city anyway, so it worked out perfect for them.

"This place is nice," Rachel said, walking into the hotel suite they were staying at for the weekend.

Rachel was a beautiful mixed woman. Her mom was Cuban and black, and her dad was black and Haitian so that gave Rachel a beautiful brown complex with Spanish features. Rachel had the brightest green eyes Sunny ever saw and her body was killing bitches like Cardi B, plus she was natural.

At twenty-four years old, she had her life together in college, a part-time job as an assistant nurse, and her own apartment. They first met at Rachel's photoshoot because she was looking into modeling. He begged her and they started dating. At first, Rachel didn't know whether to take him seriously or not until he started to invest endless time into her. Being from Baltimore, she knew a street nigga off rip, and he was that, but she loved thugs, and Sunny's thuggish ways made her fall in love.

"Happy birthday." Sunny pulled out a jewelry box with a bow tie on top of it.

"OMG, what's this?" Rachel rushed to pop the top to see the diamond necklace shining.

"You like?" Sunny saw her smile.

"I love it!" she screamed, hugging him as he grabbed her phat ass. Rachel lowered herself to the floor and unzipped his Balmain jeans, looking up at him.

"Right here?" Sunny stood in the middle of the floor.

"Ummm…" She started licking the head of his penis slowly then tried to gulp him, but unsuccessfully.

Rachel did her thing until she felt him about to explode. She took him to the bedroom and dropped her dress, showing her clean shaved kitty kat.

Sunny bent her over on the bed, not wasting time, and slid his hard-on inside of her slowly, feeling the wetness and strong grip on her walls.

The couple fucked in every position known to man and women for hours until they both tapped out, unable to keep going.

They spend most of the weekend at beaches, sightseeing, and shopping. It was the best birthday she ever had, and to have Sunny there meant so much to her.

***

Westside, B-more

Five wanted to go out and enjoy the night with his young'uns who didn't know how to act nowhere especially in public events. The hole in the wall strip club had a few nice dancers. but Five had been watching one since he pulled up in the club.

"Rolex." Five grabbed the attention of one of his shooters, who had a thick joint all over him shaking ass.

"What's good, shawty?" Rolex was an ugly young nigga with a fucked-up grill.

"Who shawty with the gold teeth and blonde hair staring at me?" Five pointed out across the room.

"Oh, that's my girl, Red Barbie," the female dancing on Rolex stated, hearing their conversation.

"Bring her over," Five demanded.

"Okay, but she about her paper," the dancer stated, looking at Five's chains and rings, knowing he had to be a big spender.

"You must not know who I am."

"Yeah, bitch, this big homie Five. We got the city on lock, blood. Now go get your homegirl," Rolex stated as the woman dashed across the room to grab her friend, who had niggas' noses wide open in the club every time she worked.

When Red Barbie came up close, Five and Rolex were gone away by the size of her pussy print.

"What's up, shawty?" Five said.

"You tell me." Red Barbie placed her arms across each other, trying to feel Five out, because she hated the broke nigga games.

"I'm trying to slide with you tonight. With all due respect, I'm trying give you a night to remember." Five spit his game.

"A night to remember could make a nigga go broke dealing with me," Red Barbie said as her homegirl slapped her hand.

"It's not enough pussy on earth to make me go broke," Five shot back

"Okay then, balla, I need 5,000 up front and 2000 when we wake up," Red Barbie said with a smirk, turning to leave, knowing a capping nigga when she saw one.

"That's all?" Five pulled out two wads of blue faces and tossed her 10,000. She caught it. "I'll meet you outside," Five said, getting up to leave to see her shocked expression.

"Can I come too?" Red Barbie's friend asked while she looked at Rolex.

"You slide with me, but I only got 2,000 for you," Rolex said.

"Shit, that will do, my pussy ain't gold," she said, excited, following Red Barbie to gather up their belongings.

Five and his crew went separate ways once their dates all came out. Red Barbie rocked a mini-dress, showing her thick tattooed-up thighs.

"We going to your place?" Red Barbie asked, putting lipstick on.

"Hell nah."

"Damn, why you say it like that? You must got a lady there?"

"Nah, I just like my privacy," he explained, driving towards downtown.

"What's your name, handsome?"

"Five."

"You getting money, I see."

"And I see you talk a lot," he replied, seeing the rude look she gave him.

"My bad. Just trying to get to know you before I suck you and let you fuck me." She poked her lip out.

“Let the money and sex do the talking,” was all Five said before texting someone at a red light

“Will do then.” She began rubbing his inner left thigh as they drove into a dangerous section she was familiar with. “I thought we was going downtown?” she asked, concerned.

“Oh, I said that?” Five sped up the car and put the child locks on.

Red Barbie got so nervous and scared she started sweating her edges out. “Where we going and can you slow down?” she was panicking now.

“Who sent you, bitch?” Five said, looking in his rearview mirror. He had seen a Chevy tail him since leaving the club.

“What are you talking about?”

Five drove into a dark block, then busted a quick right onto some small alleyway as shots could be heard from the block they were just on. Red Barbie heard the gunfire and started to cry.

“Get the fuck out!” Five’s voice rose as he got out and walked over to the passenger side door.

“No!” she screamed, seeing Five aiming a gun to her face with no other choice but to follow him.

Five dragged her into the middle of the street, where a SUV was riddled with bullet holes and a smoking hood.

“Let’s play your way.” Five opened the driver’s door to the SUV that was tailing him and saw one of the men still breathing.

Red Barbie looked at her baby father, who had put her up, to this with tears before the unthinkable happened.

BOOM!

BOOM!

BOOM!

BOOM!

Five killed Red Barbie’s baby father, then trained his gun on her.

“Okay, please, not me! A man named X put my baby father up to this. He works for him.”

Hearing X' name made Five's blood boil, causing him to put two slugs in the lady head. Five shooters all ran into different buildings with weapons at the sound of sirens. Five raced back to his car, getting the fuck away from the nasty crime scene.

When he realized the SUV was on him, Five knew it was a set-up, so he texted his goons at the red light telling them to fire on the SUV coming behind him once he got to the block.

Driving back home, Five couldn't help but laugh at the attempt on his life X had made because his enemy knew he was smarter than a regular rabbit.

Stopping at a red light, Five dialed Sunny's number to see where his nephew was at so he could tell him about the funny event.

A car shutting off its headlights smoothly pulled up on the side of him, but by the time Five reached for his weapon, it was too late.

Tat!

Tat!

Tat!

Tat!

Tat!

The black Audi drove off, rolling up its window. The driver saw a job well done as Five's head laid in the steering wheel.

***

Canaan USP, PA

Bigs entered a Puerto Rican nigga named PR's cell. PR owed him some money for drugs Bigs sold to him last week in exchange for $100 in commissary this week.

"What's popping, PR?" Bigs had an empty laundry bag in his hand, ready to collect his food and bounce.

"Yo, bro, I had to pay Romeo and Street. Can I get you next store? My mom got my money and will send however much I ask," PR stated.

"Hold on, bro, you paid the next nigga, right?"

"Yeah, but I—" PR couldn't finish his sentence before Bigs slapped the shit outta him twice. PR was already high off K-2 before Bigs entered, so the slap made him dizzy and shaky.

"I'm good for it, Bigs. When I have I not paid you?"

"Nigga, Cash App my money today by five o'clock, then get the fuck off the compound," Bigs demanded, pulling out a long blade the size of his own arm.

"Okay, okay, okay, I swear, papi, I'll get the money sent right now." PR was scared to death, seeing the sharp knife that he had witnessed Bigs stab two niggas with and get away with.

Bigs walked back to his cell pissed off. His homies saw he was mad, so they knew to leave him alone. Bigs had to roll up a blunt of weed, he was so upset. He felt played.

With only twenty months left to do, Bigs still ran around in the maximum-security jail on bullshit. He would have been home, but he lost all his good time stabbing niggas. Rags put five thousand on his account the other day and he was grateful to have a solid nigga like Rags in his corner. That was his brother for life.

Chapter 18
North Village, B-more

Sunny and Rags posted up in his crib, looking at each other in silence, both reflecting on the horrible news. When Sunny got the news, he was on his way back in town from VA with Rachel, and even she could not believe the news.

"What now?" Rags spoke up for the first time after hearing the news.

"I'm still trying to figure that out right now"

"How the fuck did they catch Unc slipping?"

"I heard Unc peeped the set-up and pulled a stunt, having the little homies on his side air out the lurkers."

"So why is he dead?" asked Rags.

"When he got a few blocks away, somebody slid up on him, doubling back."

"Damn, yo, who you think did it?" Rags really wanted to know so he could send his goons out because he had been building a little army.

"X, HD, Polo, or the police could have did the shit, so we need to be on extra point now."

"What about Unc's blocks?" asked Rags, knowing Five's little Piru homies were getting big money for Five.

"You built your crew?"

"Yeah, and they all ready."

"I need you to take over Five's blocks on the east and south, but don't forget X's and Polo's people be on the east, so it's real dangerous right now. Bodies dropping left and right. You sure you can handle it?" Sunny didn't want to get his little brother killed, but it was war time.

"Don't sleep on me."

"Everybody in life ain't meant for certain things. Rags, you're a hustler, not a killer, little bro. We all we got left out here besides Fatima, who's a cop on the good path, and we gotta kept her away from this shit."

"I agree." Rags hadn't seen or spoken to his sister since he came home, but he knew she became a cop, so Rags knew it would be best to keep his distance.

"Holla at Kanno so he can meet up with Baby Blood and them on the east so niggas can team up and do this shit right."

"I'm on it. But my people need product. We was waiting on Five."

"I know. I'ma give you the forty-two keys I have left. That should last you a few weeks until I go to Brooklyn to meet the plug since Five gone." Sunny's voice grew sad every time he thought about his uncle's slaying.

"It's no turning back now"

"Whatsoever, little bro. I love you. I'ma take Rachel home. She downstairs in the car still asleep, most likely." Sunny smiled, thinking about his boo.

"A'ight. Tell her I said hey. Be strong. We gonna get through. Did Mom or Daddy call you?" Rags asked.

"Nah, but most likely they already know," Sunny stated while walking out.

Rags had to sit down so he could let everything soak up into his head because just coming home, this was a lot. He had just built a crew with the help of Kanno and Fat P.

With Five's death, Rags was sure the Piru Bloods wanted answers, and so did the rest of the city because Five was the most loved and hated.

Tomorrow, Rags planned to explain everything to Kanno on their way to see Baby Blood, whose name in B-more was heavy like the Grim Reaper.

***

Southeast, B-more

The Maybach parked in front of Perkins Homes as groups of people admired the luxury car wondering, who was behind the dark tints. Rags had been trying to keep a low profile since being released. He knew if he was to hop out, everybody who knew him would ask for money or swing on his dick, but Rags didn't want the clout. He wanted the money. It felt good to be home where he grew up, but he didn't have nothing in common with the ghetto no more besides flooding it with drugs.

Kanno got inside the car and opened his mouth. "I'm sorry——"

"It's cool. Five knew how this shit go." Rags knew he was going to send his regards, but Rags only wanted to focus on paper.

"You right. We all got our day. But what's up ? You ready?"

"Yeah, but first we gotta go holla at Baby Blood."

"Baby Blood. For what?" Kanno got uptight and Rags peeped it.

"We about to take Five's position while everybody else teaming on snake shit."

"Who's teaming up with Baby Blood and the Piru niggas?"

"You don't like shawty?" asked Rags, feeling his boy's energy towards Baby Blood.

"Me and shawty got into a fight two years ago over a bitch we both was fucking. The only reason why I ain't bust a cap in his ass was because Five made us fight it out again."

"So it's dead?"

"I still don't like him." Kanno's face was tight.

"Bro, you tripping. We focus on a bag . Y'all niggas fighting on a bitch who gonna fuck the next dude after you and him. Look, I can't lie, that's tender dick shit. I know a nigga who would kill or fight over the next bitch is weak-minded because it was never the nigga's fault if he fucked your bitch, bro. That nigga don't owe you loyalty; she do. So don't be mad at the next man. You niggas got the game fucked up," Rags preached, seeing Kanno silent because his best friend was right.

Chapter 19
East, B-more

Baby Blood and two goons sat inside the fiend's apartment, bagging up the rest of the dog food he had left. Hearing about his big homie's death sparked rage in him and his crew. Niggas were ready to ride on whoever. Five not only showed Baby Blood the game, but he had treated the young man like his own son since day one. This morning was the first time he cried since losing his mom and dad in middle school. There was no doubt in his mind that HD or X did it because Polo and his crew weren't that crazy. Since big bro was gone, Baby Blood would have to holla at Sunny about some dog food because he still had to feed the wolves.

"Y'all niggas hurry up so we can hit the block," Baby Blood said, looking out the window to see his soldiers surrounding a clean all-white Maybach he had never seen before. He ran downstairs, telling his young'uns to stand down - all twenty of them - but they all were on point after hearing what happened with Five.

When the driver's door opened, Rags stepped out, then Kanno, but when Baby Blood saw Kanno, his face got serious, giving him a "what the fuck you want" look.

"You got a minute, Baby Blood? I'm Five's nephew," Rags said, walking around the car to embrace him.

But he wouldn't break stares with Kanno. Ray Charles could see they both still had problems with each other.

"I know who you are, Rags, and you ain't have to bring security with you." Baby Blood took a shot at Kanno, who laughed it off.

"This shit about business, yo."

"Step into my office." Baby Blood got inside his red Range Rover parked across the street.

"I know you and Five was close, but now he gone. I'ma be taking over his place, so you can fuck with me and get money as you been doing, or fuck with a opp."

Baby Blood thought about saying some fly shit back, but Rags had a valid point. The only other plugs in the city were HD, X, and Polo.

"How I know I can count on you?" Baby Blood stated.

"I'm a man of my word"

"That's what they say."

"You basically family, bro. We beefing with the same niggas and Five been feeding the whole strip since I could remember, so why not let the success continue? Now with your crew and my team together, why not take over the city?"

"You got a point. But I don't like Kanno or trust him" Baby Blood looked out his across the street at Kanno, who was leaning on the luxury car.

"I'm sure he feels the same way about you. But let me worry about Kanno. I need you to worry about getting money and finding Five's killer."

"Bet, shawty. I'm waiting on your call."

"Say no more," Rags hopped out smiling, job well done.

***

Fellas Point, B-more

Fatima woke up minutes ago from a long night of sex with her on and off boyfriend, Tavon, who she had been dealing with since college. She rarely had sex, fun, or even excitement in her life because her focus had been locked in on her career. The past weekend had been rough on her because the death of her uncle Five was being broadcast all over the news. They said a kingpin was murdered inside his car. Even though she kept a strong distance away from her family due to their criminal lifestyles, she still loved them very much. She cried all weekend. Today she planned to email her dad to tell him what happened because it was only right that he knew about his brother's loss.

Going to Five's funeral crossed her mind, then she thought against it, knowing a lot of gang members, drug dealers, killers, and law enforcement would be there. She needed to get out, so she texted her white friend Lindsey, who she went to college with. Lindsey became a federal agent for the FBI and had been making a pretty good name for herself. The two remained close friends, if not best of friends, since college.

Fatima got herself a shower, dressed, made lunch, and prepared to enjoy her Sunday before a long week of work.

***

South, B-more

Kanno really wasn't feeling the whole team up thing with Baby Blood and his Piru boys, but he knew Rags wouldn't make a bad call.

Kanno needed some gas and a box of blunts to get high because he had a lot on his mind. He drove an all-black Kia with tint, something regular, cool, and low key. He could have copped a Benz, Jaguar, or BMW, but that wasn't his style at all. Kanno loved to keep a low profile and get rich.

Walking into the store he saw a beautiful slim woman who looked familiar. Then it came to him.

"Pearla," Kanno said, remembering her from last year. She had beautiful brown skin, short curly hair, and a clean white smile.

"Oh my God, hi Kanno!" She gave him a hug. The two used to text and talk on Facebook until she went back to D.C. to finish school at Georgetown University.

"You look beautiful. How you been?"

"I'm fine. I just moved back out here. Sorry we lost contact. I was dealing with a lot, plus school."

"Trust me, it's cool. I'm glad you're back. How about you call me and we can link up over a dinner?"

"Sure, I would love that. You got the same number?"

"Yes," he replied, looking at her perky breasts.

"I'll call you later." She hugged him, slightly brushing on his penis, letting him know what time it was.

***

Downtown, B-more

X and HD met up in a UPS parking lot on a late night alone. They both came up with the idea always keeping their newfound partnership on the low. Nobody in the city would ever think two of the biggest organizations would come together.

"Job well done," HD said, extending his hand to X, smiling from ear to ear because his plan to kill Five really worked. HD had been trying to kill anybody from the Scott family for years, but never succeeded.

"I told you he would escape that set-up and fall directly into my hands," X stated.

X knew Five would realize he was being set up and make a move on the target he sent out as bait. X waited in the cut, watching the whole scene, admiring his enemy's survival tactics, but it just wasn't good enough. When X pulled up to Five, he saw his opp was lacking and gave him a round of bullets, expressing his true thoughts.

"You think they know who did it?" HD asked, hiding his nervous twitch.

"I doubt it. It's too soon. I was thinking about sending some people up to the funeral this coming weekend to send some farewell wishes," X stated.

"I think that's going be a bad idea to fuck around when the police gonna be there. Let's fall back and brainstorm on our next move." HD made sense.

"True on that indeed. Plus I have to buy some property in New Jersey this weekend for my wife to rebuild and sell," X said.

"I wonder who gonna control Five's turfs? I know them little gangbangers Five had under his wing lost now."

"Sunny most likely will take over until we kill him," X added.

"I been thinking about that Polo kid. Maybe we should try to recruit him with us," HD threw out.

"I've heard good things about the kid, but he is not a seasoned vet. He is young and partly new to the game. I don't know where he even came from."

"Just a thought."

"I'ma plot a new mission out soon. Until then, let's take what's ours," X said.

"The life we earned." HD laughed.

***

South B-more
Days later

Rags raced through the main blocks in the south section of the town, trying to make it to his uncle's funeral on time. Rags ended up falling asleep real late after dropping off Kanno and Baby Blood the kilos of heroin, a.k.a. dog food, he got from Sunny.

After the funeral, Sunny stated he needed to speak to him, Rags saw it in a text this morning. Rags hated funerals and weddings. For some reason, he had always been very uncomfortable in those types of settings.

Yesterday he had a chance to speak with his father, who was very displeased with Five's death. Proof told Rags to try and become a better man than him and his late uncle. Since being released, Rags had a few plans he was about to achieve in a matter of days. One was real estate.

Rags saw that when there was a lot of dirty money laying around and nobody had a business to clean up the money, then it can become a waste in the wrong person's hands. His papa was a firm believer in that. Seeing his dad and mom own so many businesses, he used to wonder what the real reason for it was. Now he understood the logic behind it.

Rags ran a red light, unaware of the cop parked on the corner until the police car threw on its lights.

"Shit!" Rags pulled over, placing his gun inside the glove compartment. He already had his license and paperwork in the sun visor. A beautiful black woman approached the car in sunglasses because it was so bright outside today.

"May I have your—" The cop paused. "Doug?" She took off her shades so he could see her face.

"Fatima? What the fuck? You look different. I'm so proud of you," Rags said, looking at his sister's uniform.

"Thanks and welcome home. What you plan to do?"

"Well, I got my real estate license so I'ma buy some houses and buildings to flip." Rags didn't want to tell her he was back in the game because she would have been disappointed and she was still a cop in his eyes.

"Yes, stay on the right path, brother. I'm sorry to hear about Uncle Five. It really touched me. But these streets are very dangerous right now," she stated.

"I'm on the way to the funeral now."

"Okay, well, be safe, and regardless of this uniform, I love you."

"I love you too, sis." Rags really loved his sis, but jail time and the streets grew them apart. They used to be so close.

Chapter 20
Monument east, B-more

Marcus played basketball at the rec center on the east side every Monday with his homies. Being in college only gave him two days out of the week to have fun, which was Sunday and Monday because he had no classes.

At nineteen years old, he was a very handsome, intelligent kid with a good head on his shoulders. His father X raised him correctly, even though he barely came around due to the street life, but Marcus loved his pops very much.

Since he was a child, X always pushed him to go get educated so he could become a doctor, lawyer, or even a police officer. As a kid, Marcus soaked it all up. Now he was becoming a lawyer with two years left of law school.

"Man, y'all suck. We lost by two points, bro. You should have passed me the ball!" Marcus yelled to his friend Chewy, whom he had known since they were kids.

"Maybe. I ain't see you, bro. My mind been elsewhere," Chewy said, packing up his water bottle in his gym bag.

"What's wrong? You straight?" Marcus seemed concerned because he peeped that Chewy had been acting weird the last few weeks.

"My girl pregnant."

"What? Since when? Wow, bro, I'm happy for you." Marcus wondered why Chewy's expression was sour.

"I don't know if it's mines or not, bro. Ashley told me it could be some nigga named Sha or Kanno," Chewy stated, holding in his disappointment.

"Hold on. She was fucking all three of y'all?" Marcus heard Ashley was a big-time freak, but he ain't know she was a savage.

"Come on, Marcus, don't make it sound more worse than it already is."

"My bad. But don't stress that, bro. Fuck her, my nigga, just get a DNA." Marcus just suggested something that had been heavy on Chewy's mind.

"I am, trust me. I have no choice whatsoever" Chewy stated leaving the rec center.

It was dark outside, but the night was still young for both men.

"You trying hit up a club later? I heard Lil Durk coming to the city." Marcus hoped to brighten his boy's day.

"Let me call me mom first to see if she can Cash App me some money," he stated

A car appeared from a parking spot and pressed the gas, running right into Chewy, knocking him down.

"Yo, what the fuck?" Marcus tried to help his friend up off the ground. Then the driver slowly climbed out.

Bloc! Bloc! Bloc! Bloc!

Bullets quickly found their way into Chewy's skull, killing him. A van pulled up and two masked men grabbed Marcus off the floor. Marcus was numb to what he just saw, so he didn't put up a fight, a scream, or a cry for help as the men tossed him into the van.

Rags climbed back into the car Kanno's side bitch rented and followed the van to the secret location.

Sunny told Rags after the funeral he had the drop on X's son, a young nigga named Marcus who was in college and came down to a local rec center every Monday to play ball. Rags come up with a retaliation plot to even the scoreboard.

It didn't take long for the gang to make it over to Perkin Homes. There was a downstairs laundry room in one of the buildings they trapped out of day and night. The area was pitch black and nobody was out, so it all worked out.

Kanno and Fat P took Marcus out of the van, quickly escorting him inside the back of a rundown building with no cameras anywhere around. Rags followed after them checking the area to make sure everything was good even though Perkins Homes was the most dangerous hood in the southeast everybody was used to violence.

"Should we tie him to the bars in them windows?" Fat P pointed towards the steel bars.

"No, let him go. Kanno, hold the door down," Rags spoke calmly, approaching the scared Marcus, who was shaking in fear.

"I'm not about this life. Whatever took place with my dad doesn't concern me. I'm a college kid, please!" Marcus cried fearing for this day.

"You know we here for X, huh?" Rags said, now face to face with the kid.

"Well, you are, right? There could be no other reason. I don't have a girl because I'm gay." Marcus saw Fat P give him a nasty look.

"What can you tell me about X?"

"I barely see my dad. He be with his new wife or traveling."

"I'ma need a address."

"He just moved last week," Marcus lied trying to save his father.

Rags shot him in both feet for lying as he cried out in pain, falling to the ground.

"A little less lies," Fat P said, laughing.

"I swear I don't know, bro. The only thing I do know is on some weekends he likes to go gamble in Atlantic City or D.C."

"Kill him and toss him in the dryer. I'ma be outside." Rags walked out, pleased with the new info he got. He didn't know if X killed Five or not, nor did he care.

Chapter 21
Outskirts, B-more

X woke up to his beautiful wife tapping him.

"Baby, somebody knocking on the front door," Jena said nervously.

X looked over at the alarm clock that read 3:15 a.m. He made sure only two or three people knew where he lived at for safety purposes. He climbed outta bed and made his way downstairs, looking out his glass front door. He saw two uniformed cops, a young lady and a young white cop who looked impatient.

"What the fuck?" X got in panic mood wondering if the Five killing got linked back to him.

"Sorry for waking you up, sir, but this young man was found murdered this evening and this is the address we found on his ID," the white cop stated, handing X the ID.

When X saw it was his son's ID, his knees almost went out on him as Jena was racing downstairs.

"Is everything okay, baby?" Jena looked over X's shoulder at the pretty young lady and the racist-looking young cop.

"Someone killed Marcus." X couldn't believe it as tears filled his eyes.

"We know it's a bad time. Once again, sorry for your loss, but we do need you to come identify the body," Fatima said in a soft voice, feeling sad for the man and his family.

"Okay, give us an hour," Jena spoke up for X, who was at a loss for words. She closed the door in the police's face and let her husband mourn over his son's death.

***

Brooklyn, NY

Sunny had only been to New York three times in his life but he will be lying if he says New York wasn't one of his favorite places.

He wasn't out in downtown Brooklyn on a sightseeing trip. Instead, he had to meet up with his cousin, whom he never met. The only thing Sunny knew was that people on his dad's side of the family were all mainly African and rich. Proof never really talked about that side of the family, so Sunny never pushed the issue.

Five gave Sunny a number months ago and told him if anything ever happened to him to call that number and he would be set. The Africans already knew who were all close kin to Proof.

This would be the first time Sunny met the plug, so he was a little nervous, but he would be taking Five's spot, so Sunny knew he would soon be used to it. Word on the street was that X's and HD's people seemed to be cheering over Five's death. Sunny wanted to put his focus on chasing the money, but with so much beef, it made shit hard to focus on one thing.

The plug texted Sunny an address and a time, but the location was at a bookstore, Barnes & Noble. Sunny acted as if he was reading a book called *Chiraq Gangstas*.

A young brother wearing glasses sat down to read a book. He looked no older than twenty-five. He was clean cut with a nerdy look.

"Pardon me, bro, but I'm waiting on someone. Do you mind using another table?" Sunny respectfully asked.

"You look just like uncle Proof," the young man replied while reading a self-help book calmly.

"Oh shit, it's you I'm waiting on?" Sunny would never imagine the kid to be a plug.

"Unless you waiting on Jesus," he shot back with a laugh.

"Nice to meet you."

"Same here. I'm sorry for what happened to Uncle Five. My dad is very angry about that and hopes the fam out there is capable of letting Five's soul rest on revenge." The young brother looked his cousin Sunny in his eyes.

"Of course. My little brother is on it as we speak," Sunny claimed.

"Rags just came home, right?"

"Yeah, how did you know?" Sunny knew the cat had heard of him, but Rags too?

"We had people in Big Sandy looking over him. We family, Sunny, just a different type of bond. Our family reunions is this business. Tell Rags Cory and Big Black send their regards to him."

"Sure. But what's your name anyway?"

"North."

"A'ight, so now Five gone, how we gonna do this shit?"

"The same way. We will meet up here once a month every 15th unless the plans happen to change or something goes wrong, but you will be informed of any change of plans." North looked at two white girls who were smiling at him so he smiled back.

"I got it."

"There will be a car loaded with your drugs parked not too far from your car, and my people will follow you back to B-more. If they happen to get pulled over, my people will not stop. You understand they will try to get away or shoot it out. We from Brooklyn, son."

"I like you already." Sunny smiled, ready to head back.

"One last thing. Never cross us," North said before disappearing.

Chapter 22
Eastside B-more

Fat P left a little bitch's crib named D Baby, who had a mean head game and her pussy was splashing, but the only thing was the smell. D Baby's coochie smelled like horse shit on a hot day, but niggas couldn't leave her alone.

As he walked out of the lobby of her building, a few niggas posted up, hanging out, but Fat P continued to walk and mind his business. Outside, he almost stepped on a nigga telling wars stories to impress some young cats.

"Damn, fat ass." The young man looked up at Fat P, who almost fell over him. The nigga had seen Fat P somewhere before, but it wasn't coming to him.

"No need for name calling, shawty. My bad, you hear me?" Fat P walked off, shaking his head.

"You look like you got some fly shit to say." The young man rose up with five members of his crew.

"I'm just trying to slide home, shawty." Fat P saw the goons surround him as he got into the street light, then he recognized the nigga popping shit. It was Sha.

Fat P wasn't about to go out like no bitch, so he pulled out his Glock 19 and fired wildly.

Boc! Boc! Boc! Boc! Boc! Boc! Boc!

Two of Sha's people got shot while most of them tried to run, except Sha, who fired back.

Bloc! Bloc! Bloc! Bloc!

Fat P felt a burn in his left arm once he made it to his car. Bullets were now coming from everywhere, hitting Fat P's car as he drove off.

"Bitch-ass niggas." Fat P drove himself back to the hood. At one point, he pulled over to check on his bleeding wound to see how bad it was. He thought the bullet was still inside of him, but it had exited through the other side of his arm, so he was good.

Fat P didn't knows too much about Sha besides the fact that he worked with Polo, who he barely knew.

Pulling up on the southeast section, he drove right to Perkins Homes, where niggas were still out hustling. Kanno was posted in the front with fifty little shooters, ready to take off anybody's head.

"What the fuck happened to you?" asked Kanno, seeing Fat P get out of his car, wrapping a T-shirt around his bloody arm in pain.

"I was fucking with D Baby—"

"Oh nah, dude, I told you she burnt the little homie last week." Kanno knew Fat P was a horny nigga, but there was too many bitches for him to be tripping over dirty pussy.

"Nigga, listen, I been burnt a few times. I don't care. But listen, I'm leaving her crib high as hell and niggas start saying little comments outside, but I'm trying slide out his way. One of them little niggas got up popping big shit as they surrounded me, and you know what I did." Fat P placed two fingers in the air.

"Who was the dude?" Kanno knew the area D Baby lived in belonged to Polo, a nigga he hated.

"Sha."

"We about to slide on them hoe-ass niggas." Kanno was heated because outta all them cats he hated Sha the most.

"Nah, they block hot, shawty. I may have just laid something down," Fat P said as one of their shooters Devin approached them.

"Yo, niggas saying two bodies just dropped on Sha's block and Fat P did it," Devin said, just getting off the phone with a bitch from over there.

"You see? Already." Fat P was tight because someone would snitch if they didn't already, and going to jail for bodies wasn't on his to do list.

"Bro, you gotta get outta town." Kanno knew anytime word spread that fast, somebody told the police something and someone was going to jail.

"I'ma go to my sister's crib in VA for a few weeks." Fat P knew Kanno was right.

"A'ight, here take this." Kanno handed him two wads of money.

"Love you, bro." Fat P gave Kanno a hug.

"Love you too. Call me when you get there, yo," Kanno said as Fat P jumped back in his four door Charger and headed down to VA.

***

North Village, B-more

"I'ma have all your bread from the product you already gave me. Kanno got like eight keys left. He said the junkies loved it," Rags told Sunny, who had just dropped off another 40 keys.

"Keep that money. Trust me, we got an unlimited supply now. The plug is fam and good people so we straight. He also mentioned you," Sunny stated, recounting the product on the living room table.

"Me?"

"Yeah. He said Cory and Big Black send their regards or some shit."

Rags knew who the two ruthless African men were. They were in his unit in jail and always looked out for him, even though they were both from Brooklyn, NY doing life bids.

"Okay, those were my guys. I fuck wit' my BK niggas," Rags said, staring at the tan kilo.

Chapter 23
East B-more

Polo waited for Sha to come outside from his baby mother's crib to see what the emergency was because Polo had been down in Atlanta with his cousins for the past few days.

Coming back to the city, he knew niggas needed product, so that was first on his mind. Before coming over here, he picked up ten keys of dope from his side bitch's crib.

The recent news of Five's death made Polo celebrate because now he could move into his old blocks. Polo's main focus was to take over as much block as possible. Even though his strips did numbers, Polo was the greedy type.

Sha came out of the building on the quiet block, seeing the black Audi Q3 truck that belonged to his friend.

"Welcome back." Sha was being funny, and Polo caught on.

Polo had known Sha long enough to know when he was upset about something and when he was ready to kill. "We all deserve a breath of fresh air, wouldn't you agree?" Polo questioned, but the look on Sha's face said it all.

"You missed out."

"On what?" Polo hated problems. He was about money, but he would turn up when he needed to be.

"Kanno's cousin Fat P came through here on bullshit and one thing led to another, bro."

"What happened, nigga? Get to the point," Polo hated when Sha stalled out.

"He killed Juice and Fly Tee."

"My cousin Juice?"

"Yeah. He died in a coma two days ago. I'm sorry, bro." Sha knew how much Polo loved Juice. He basically raised the sixteen-year-old himself.

"It's war now, yo."

Sha was surprised at Polo's reaction because he wasn't the violent type. Sha handled all of the street drama and pushed the buttons.

"You sure?"

"Yeah. And spin the block on Fat P every day until you find him." Polo was on fire.

"It's no turning back now, bro." Sha smiled.

"Facts. And I want you to take over Five's block where them Piru niggas be at, shawty."

"Baby Blood's crazy ass runs that shit now," Sha shot back.

"Fuck him. Take that shit over, bro. Send a message and let them know we did it," Polo stated.

Sha couldn't believe this was coming out of Polo's mouth, but he was liking it a lot.

***

Downtown, B-more

Carena had attended her first DA meeting minutes ago on the 13th floor with all the top bosses. The meeting was basically about up and coming federal indictments the FBI had brewing, and number one was the Tree Top Pirus on the east side of B-more. The main target, her boss explained, was a man named Five who was murdered by a rival, the feds believed, because of the city drug war going on. Since the head boss was out of the picture, the feds believe a young man named Baby Blood was going to replace the late kingpin.

When Carena heard Five's last name - Scott - she got chills, knowing Rags' last name was Scott. All types of thoughts flooded her mind, and she became concerned for Rags safety and well-being.

Getting back to her small office, Carena looked into the Piru caseload, mainly at Five, to see what the federal government had on him. Carena spent two hours going through caseload relating to Five and she couldn't believe her eyes. The feds had seven unsolved murders they believed to be done by Five and his crew within the last year. There were no solid evidence; only a lot of serious assumptions, but no witnesses, DNA, or footage.

She was glad Rags had no ties to Five's case, but she wondered who Five was to him. Carena saw no connection at all, which made her believe Rags really had changed his life.

Tired of looking over paperwork, she took a lunch break.

***

South B-more

Pearla looked at the way her new dress fit her slim, nice curves and wanted to dance. She figured going to the gym five days a week wasn't doing it until now when she finally put that designer shit on.

Tonight, she and Kanno were going on a dinner date downtown. This would be her first real date and she was more than happy because most niggas just wanted to fuck and move on. Every night she would stay up late talking to Kanno. Even though she knew he was in the streets, she didn't care.

Pearla had ,just landed a job as a correctional officer at the county jail. She had been waiting for a few months to land the job so she was happy. Her brother, Sean P, was supposed to take her out to celebrate but she canceled for her date with Kanno.

Chapter 24
Downtown B-more

Rags borrowed a car from Kanno's people because he couldn't use his Maybach for what he had planned tonight on his lurk. Rags was very pleased with the product. Sunny said it was a lot better than the recent work Five was getting. Sunny started to think Five was cutting the product before Sunny got to it because it was never this strong. Rags didn't know how to reply, but he said Five wouldn't do that. He sat in the parked car, watching customers walk in and out of the car dealership as they were about to close for the night.

For some reason, Carena had been popping up in his head constantly. He'd be lying if he said he didn't miss her now and during his whole bid in jail. Rags scrolled to social media, searching for Carena's page to see what she had been up to. Rags feared he would see something that hurt him, like Carena having kids, being married, or looking bad. When he saw Carena, he couldn't believe how beautiful and thick she got over the last few years. Rags saw pics of her graduating college, vacations pics, and pictures of her on a beach looking sexy.

"Damn, gurl," Rags mumbled, feeling himself get horny. He wanted to slide in her DMs or like one of her pictures, but he couldn't bring himself to do it.

Rags' attention shifted back on his mission as he saw the white man he had been stalking all day. Since Rags had a little free time on his hands, he wanted to start buying a few properties to sell, putting the real estate licenses he got in jail to use. He also wanted to take care of the person who killed his uncle Five, and word on the streets was that X and HD had something to do with it. Sunny told him the people they were up against weren't normal street punks, but Rags didn't give a fuck. He wanted payback.

Climbing out of the Saturn sedan, he smoothly walked to the dealership in a suit and tie.

***

Jack had a long day dealing with ungrateful customers and he was ready to go home to his family. Running a car dealership was a headache, especially with only four dumb employees. HD didn't know how to run a business, so Jack ran it and HD funded it, which was a perfect exchange. Jack never questioned HD's whereabouts dealing with the income. Jack just wanted his big phat check every week.

Jack saw a young man banging on the glass, but he had just closed sixty seconds ago.

"Go away. We closed, asshole!" Jack shouted, seeing the young man in the suit continue to bang. "Fucker." Jack went to the main entrance, using his key to open the door. "We're fucking closed, kid," Jack stated

"How about we have a nice talk real quick?"

"Get the fuck——" Jack paused when the man raised a gun into Jack face.

"Step back inside, bitch nigga," Rags stated.

"Okay. Relax." Jack lifted his hands as he backed up, fearing for God.

"Stop right there, playboy. Have a seat, hoe nigga, because I been watching you and you're in in business with HD."

"Who is that?" Jack played dumb.

The butt of Rags' gun knocked out two teeth and he spit blood out.

"One more time. HD…where can I find him?" Rags got in Jack's face, putting a gun to his head.

"Chill, man. All I know is he got a nice mansion in Georgetown, D.C. I believe his baby mother and kids live there."

"What street?"

"Water Avenue or Union Street, one of those. I swear, he moves like a ghost. I barely see him coming or going, man." Jack bit his lip and wanted to cry.

Bloc!

Bloc!

Bloc!

Rags had enough information for him to put a plan together, so he felt like it was a job well done.

***

Norfolk, VA

Fat P hated coming to Norfolk because there wasn't anything for him to do besides smoke, drink, and fuck bitches in his sister's projects area.

Kanno told him he should be good to come back in a few weeks because the two bodies that dropped had been reported on the news as an unsolved case. There was so much shit going on back home and Fat P wanted a piece of it, plus he didn't feel right leaving Kanno and Rags alone back home. Fat P knew they had a bunch of goons on deck for war, but Fat P was the top shoota.

He got up and walked to the store to grab some wraps for his weed and saw a bunch of country niggas with old school cars sitting on big rims.

"Country bumpkins," he mumbled, walking to the store, but someone overheard him.

"What you say, bruh?" a tall, dark-skinned nigga said, hopping off the hood of his car.

"Nigga, if I would have said something to you, then you would have heard it," Fat P shot back.

"You must don't know where the fuck you at, my nigga."

"To be real, I don't give a fuck. I'm 'bout that life." Fat P was now face to chest with dude because he stood 6'5" over Fat P's 5'6" frame.

The man reached back and slapped the fire outta Fat P and turned to walk away, laughing to two women waiting on him.

Fat P pulled out a weapon, not thinking twice.

Boc!

Boc!

Boc!

Boc!

Boc!

Fat P shot the tall man in the back of his head twice and shot one of the chicks with him before running off in broad daylight. He lived sixty feet away from the crime scene.

***

Downtown, B-more

“Georgetown in D.C., huh?” Sunny said, repeating what his little brother just told him as they drove around looking for buildings to purchase. Rags already had the contact information for three spots he wanted to look into.

“Yeah. I’m ready to slide out there with the guys.” Rags hadn’t slept since he gathered HD’s location from the late Jack.

“Nah, wait, because dude and X gonna be on point. They’re probably trying to plot some shit together. Shit, you just killed X’s son and HD’s white boy,” Sunny explained.

“Maybe you right. I didn't expect them to come together, but it’s smart.”

“Only God knows. But only time will tell,” Sunny said, turning up the car stereo.

Chapter 25
South, B-more

X exited the church, leaving his son's funeral on his way to bury him in the same graveyard as X's brothers, uncles, and dad. He haven't seen a church in years since he was a little kid, and he prayed this would be the last time.

Family and friends of Marcus flooded the church lot, mourning. X saw a black Cadillac truck full of goons with HD standing in front of it.

"Sorry about your loss, big bro. My respect goes out, slim," HD said, seeing X's woman right by his side, and he could tell she was the classy, boss bitch type.

"Thank you. My son didn't deserve this."

"I know. But you got a second in private?" asked HD.

"I'ma meet you at the car," X told his wife, who walked away, giving HD a nasty look. There was something about him she didn't like at all.

"Someone killed my business partner at my car dealership, X. They onto us." HD got nervous, walking away from his SUV.

"Damn, they figured it out," X mumbled, wondering if it was a bad idea to team up with HD because now, somehow, word got out they took Five's life.

"Figured what out, slim?"

"That we working together, because they coming at us both."

"That's why I'm riding with my security wherever I go from now on."

"I think I'ma do the same," X stated, feeling like this was only a taste of what was coming.

"We need to have another sit down and plot something out quick for Sunny."

"I agree. This weekend coming up, I'll give you a call," X said.

"Okay," HD replied before climbing back into the SUV and driving off.

X knew Sunny wasn't bright enough to make all this shit happen and Proof was in prison doing life, so he felt like there had to be something missing from the puzzle.

X got back with his wife to go bury their son and reflect on the memories they did have with Marcus.

***

West, B-more

Dozen leaned back in his seat, watching Sean P hug and kiss on a young lady who had his son in her arms. Dozen never knew Sean P had a baby boy, but he wrote down the address just in case someone needed it.

The past few weeks since his brother's death, he had been cleaning up the mess Rags and his crew had been leaving behind, especially the Fat P situation. If it wasn't for Dozen, then Fat P would be in jail because Dozen forced a witness to pick out the wrong shooter and write statements. Two people from Sha's crew tried to say they saw Fat P do the shooting which killed two of their friends. Dozen ended up throwing a gun in one of their cars and arresting him an hour later. The other witness, Dozen caught him in an alley two nights ago having sexual intercourse with a little girl who was only fourteen years old. The man was shocked. He stated she told him her age was eighteen. But Dozen locked him up anyway.

Last night, he met up with Rags, who hit him off with three kilos of dope, and Dozen took it right to his people in New Jersey. Rags was family, so he didn't have to pay. Dozen got enough drugs and money from local drug dealers.

When he peeped Sean P walk to his car, Dozen made his move, getting out of the undercover car.

"My boy Sean P." Dozen shocked him by coming from his blind side.

"What the fuck you want, pig?"

"Funny. I like you, little nigga, but that won't stop me from putting a bullet in you."

"I don't talk to police, so whatever you gotta say, slip it." Sean P leaned on his car, already knowing what type of nigga Dozen was: grimy and low down.

"Word on the street is you're the one who killed that kid Five."

"Who is that?" Sean P played dumb.

"Oh, you know, because there is a nice bounty on your head out here, and I been seeing a lot of little hungry niggas running around."

"If there was a bounty on my head, why would that concern you?"

"Because how I see it is, we can help each other. I know people that know people." Dozen gave him a wink.

"I'd rather die than go to a pig for help and you know what makes you the worst? You're worse than a pig. You're a fuckin *hog*!"

Sean P didn't see it coming, but Dozen cocked his right fist back and broke Sean P's nose.

"Hold that, little nigga, and do something. I'll blow your fucking brains out with a reasonable cause." Dozen saw blood leak all over Sean P's Armani shirt.

"You got that." Sean P rushed inside the car, holding his nose.

"If you need me, you know where I'm at, Sean P. The police station," Dozen stated, hoping someone heard him.

Sean P dipped off, pissed, ready to kill Dozen, but he was the police. He had no wins.

Chapter 26
Downtown, B-more
Next day

Today was a big day for Rags. He was about to buy his first house to flip. On the Southside in a middle-class area, he got ahold of a nice two-story building with two levels and a front and back yard.

Rags felt like he was financially achieving something positive in life by doing real estate. He planned to invest most of his money into homes and apartment buildings. Sunny wanted to go half with him, but Rags respectfully declined because he had more than enough money to buy the properties.

"My tie." Rags realized he forgot to put on a tie with his fitted gray suit. To the right of him, he saw a small shopping center with a few clothing stores, so he quickly found a parking spot. He saw Marshall's and was making his way inside until he heard someone call his government name.

"Doug!" a female voice shouted from behind him.

When he turned around, Rags couldn't believe his eyes. Carena looked more beautiful than he could remember, so he was speechless for a second. "Carena, nice to see you." Rags liked how professional and classy she looked in her business suit for women, and they both had on the same color.

"Welcome home. How you been?" He looked with his long dreads and masculine frame.

"Thanks, and I'm blessed, doing real estate, about to open up my first house today to resell."

"Real estate? Wow." Carena couldn't believe her ears. He really turned his life around she was proud.

"I wanna apologize for my actions during my bid because I know you only had good intentions for me." He sounded very sincere.

"It's okay. We all go through things in life. But look at you now. You bossed up."

"It took my sentence for me to really open my eyes."

"I guess that's life. I'm a new face to the DA here in the Baltimore federal court system," she said.

"Hold on. You're a DA?" Rags couldn't believe his ears.

"Yes. I went to college so I could become one. I wanted to tell you, but we split apart," she said sadly.

"I'm proud of you, Carena. I always knew you would be something special in life. I'm surprised you're not married to some big-time lawyer or doctor." He tried to fish to check on her relationship status.

"Oh hell no! Dudes out here ain't on my level or worth my time, plus I'm so focused on my career right now," she made clear.

"That's the best thing for you. I feel the same way."

"Do you have that someone special?"

"Nah. I'm gay."

"WHAT!" She almost lost control of herself.

"I'm just joking, calm down." Rags started to laugh as she took deep breaths.

"You can't play like that these days. Half of these guys are bi-sexual, confused, or gay."

"I love women too much"

"I bet you do." She gave him a look.

"My broker should be waiting on me. Can we finish this conversation a little later?"

"Sure. Why not take my personal number?" Carena and Rags switched numbers before parting ways.

Rags rushed to buy a black and gray tie, thinking how crazy life worked because running into Carena was the last thing on his mind. To hear her position as a federal DA made him nervous. He knew there was no way she could find out about his life outside of real estate.

Seeing how good she looked made him regret splitting up with her but at the same time, he didn't want to hold Carena back from her life.

***

East, Baltimore

“Five bundles and up. If your dusty ass can’t afford it, then go up the block,” LB told a dope fiend who approached him with crumpled money adding up to a hundred and fifty dollars. A bundle on LB’s block went for fifty cash and he only sold five bundles at a time. Each bundle had ten small bags of dog food inside and you could sell each for ten dollars apiece.

“Up the block, they have better dope. Your bullshit only gets me high for an hour. Baby Blood’s shit have me high and nodding all day.”

The man turned to walk off until LB grabbed him by the back of his. shirt slamming him to the floor. LB started pistol-whipping the man in front of a group of fiends and drug dealers who worked for him and his brother Polo. LB loved the streets: selling drugs, the shootouts, and everything that comes with it.

“Talk that shit now!” LB yelled as he beat the fiend lifeless.

People shook their heads at LB’s action because dope head Freddy used to be a big-time drug lord in his days and people loved him.

“Get rid of this piece of shit,” LB told two of his workers before walking up the block to get rid of the murder weapon.

LB stopped in a dark alley to put the bloody weapon into the dumpster, then closed it. When he turned around, a Colt 45 handgun was in his face.

“LB, send Polo and dem a message for us, yo,” said Kanno.

Bloc!

Bloc!

Bloc!

Kanno ran out the alley and up the block to safety, hearing sirens from all over as he got low on a dirt bike back to southeast, taking the back blocks.

Chapter 27
Downtown, Baltimore

Fatima day was very long and she was more than exhausted. Her on and off boyfriend Tavon wanted to take Fatima out to dinner, but there was no way she could go without falling asleep on the table. Fatima respectfully declined. She just wanted to hit the bed to prepare for the next day.

As she walked through the building, one of her captains approached her with a big smile. "How you doing in the field, Ms. Scott?" Captain White asked. He had over two decades on the force.

"It's going great. Just getting used to it"

"That's good. By any chance do you happen to be related to the notorious Scott family?"

"No sir, I've never heard of them. My family is all from Texas and Chicago." Fatima's palms got sweaty.

"Alright then, but if you don't know who the Scott family is, young lady, you better do your research. Those fuckers are the real deal. The majority of the city murder cases and drug trafficking comes from them. We could never bust them smart bastards, but luckily, the feds took down Proof and his wife. Boy, that was big. I celebrated." Captain White smiled, but the look on Fatima's face was serious.

"I got work to do. I'll see you around, Captain," Fatima said before turning to walk off.

"Will do, will do." Captain White watched her walk away, thinking about why the young lady's face looked so familiar. He walked off, not trying to bust his brain.

There had been so much crime in the city lately. His station had been heavy with murder cases and assaults. He couldn't remember the last time the city turned into a war zone, but he had all his best cops on it, trying to find the key players, and he knew the Scott family was in the mix. With Proof locked up and Five dead and stanking, he knew the only person who could be running the show was Sunny and the Piru Bloods his uncle Five had groomed.

A few days ago, he got a report from the FBI building a case on the Piru's members. A new DA named Carena Rizzio was leading the case and he hoped she nailed all of those low lives, especially Baby Blood, who shot one of his cops two years ago and got away with it.

***

PG County, B-more

Sean P had a magnificent mini mansion with beautiful interior design all throughout the spot. The landscaping in the front and back looked amazing. Inside, he had four reception rooms, four bedrooms, a swimming pool, a gated driveway parking, and an annex. Only a few people knew where he lived and mainly, those people were family and close friends.

The weather was so nice today that he threw a cook-out in his backyard, inviting family. They played music and games, drank, smoked, and cooked on his large grills.

"Pearla, what you doing, little sis?" Sean P saw his sister pouring herself a glass of Henny. She was never really a drinker before she went back to D.C. to finish college. Sean P was proud of his sister. She meant everything to him.

"Getting my sip on. What it look like?" she replied, laughing.

"What you been up to? Because I'm not feeling how you curved our get together last week"

"My bad. I was on a date."

"You dating?" He seemed shocked because she always talked about how niggas weren't shit.

"Yeah. I went to school with him. He's a good dude."

"What's his name?"

"Damn, nosy."

"Just for safety measures." Sean P didn't wanna tell her he had a lot of opps, so he kept it rated G.

"If you must know, his name is Jermaine from southeast."

"Southeast? Be careful over there," he warned her.

"I don't be over there, Sean, I got a life," she stated, taking a sip of Henny.

Sean P knew his sister would never give a street nigga like him her time, so he had no concerns. He just wanted to see her happy and focused on her success. "Any vacations for this summer? I know your birthday coming up."

"I wanna go to Jamaica. Me and my boo," she replied.

"Damn, yo' boo already? You moving a little too fast, don't you think?"

"Nope, perfect. But I'm going to get me a plate, playa." Pearla tapped her brother on his chest, walking off, shaking the red dreads she recently put in her hair.

Chapter 28
Eastside, B-more

"Park right there, shawty," Sha told the driver of the minivan. He pointed to an empty space at the end of a dangerous block they nicknamed 400 block for all the Piru gang members that were there.

Sha and his goons spun the block, looking for Baby Blood, but they only saw fiends and soldiers out tonight.

"We should light this whole block up for the big bro," Squeeze said from the backseat.

Since LB's murder, Polo and Sha had been in their bag, ready to kill the whole city over LB's death. When Sha heard Baby Blood and Kanno became allies, he knew shit would get worse before better, so coming up with a plan to take out Baby Blood and then Kanno was established.

"If we don't see this goofy little nigga in five minutes, we gonna make this shit look like an early 4th of July," Sha told his four-man crew, who were all carrying big military assault rifles.

***

Across the street

"Yo, I'm telling you, Blood, that's him," Country said, peeping out the crack in the boarded-up window of the abandoned house with twenty goons inside, strapped and thirsty for any type of action.

Baby Blood's little niggas saw Sha in the passenger seat of a van circling the block, looking for someone. Baby Blood watched the minivan at the end of the corner.

"Look, I want ten of y'all to go out the back way and creep around the block and creep up behind the van. The rest of you, come with me. Let's put on a movie, yo." Baby Blood walked out through the side door, leading into an alleyway.

***

"There he go." Sha smiled, seeing Baby Blood and a gang of niggas with him coming out the alley, walking towards them.

"I'm ready," Squeeze said, checking the switch on his Draco.

"They fell right into our hands," another soldier stated.

"Yeah, which is a little odd, but fuck it, they slipping. Come on, show no mercy, shawty," Sha said as they hopped out of the van and his goons followed.

Before they could let off one round, bullets surprised them from behind.

Tat!

Tat!

Tat!

Boc!

Boc!

Boc!

BOOM!

Squeeze's body jerked with bullets before hitting the pavement as everybody else took cover and fired back. Sha saw Baby Blood and the rest of his crew about to block them in, so he looked around and saw a park.

Tat! Tat! Tat! Tat! Tat! Tat!

Another one of Sha's goons got riddled with bullets. Without thinking twice, Sha took off running into the dark park, not knowing he had already been hit in his left upper thigh. The rest of Sha's crew didn't stand a chance as they got slaughtered.

***

Downtown, B-more
Days later

The downtown section of Baltimore was large. The area had a lot of sky rise buildings, restaurants, clubs, boardwalks, hotels, banks, and shopping areas.

Rags and Carena had finally made arrangements to go out to eat tonight and they had a good time. Now they were both seated by the water, enjoying the night view and stars.

"When I was a kid, I always wanted to go in the sky just to see what was there," Carena said, looking at all the bright stars.

"What's stopping you?"

"I don't know. Life, work, and doubt that I will ever get the chance to," she explained. It started to get a little chilly and he gave her his Louis Vuitton sweater. "Thank you," she said, putting the warm fabric over her dress.

"I dream a lot these days, especially when I was locked up. Every night, I had a dream," Rags admitted.

"About what?" She cuddled up next to him, which surprised him.

"Just life - living a good, perfect life."

"You somewhat have that now, and you just came home. Some people been out of prison five to ten years and still lost out here. That's why they go back. But you're different. You followed your goals and visions"

"I mean, I guess. But I wanna do more to help others."

"Sometimes, if people can't do for themselves, there is only so much someone else can do for them," she told him.

"Facts. But I want to be in a position to help everybody succeed."

"I understand. But I gotta go. It's getting late and I got work at 5 a.m. Text me in the morning." She gave him his sweater back then a light kiss on the lips.

Chapter 29
Westside, B-more

Lauren almost ran a red light, she was so pissed off. A good friend of hers sent pictures and screenshots of Sean P saying he loved her. What sealed the deal was when Lauren saw pictures of him eating the lady who used to be her best friend's pussy. Her friend stated she couldn't deal with the guilt, so she had to come clean, but Lauren hated the bitch for fucking the love of her life and child's father. She hadn't slept in days, plotting ways to get him back, and Lauren came up with the idea of death.

Sean P used to tell her about all his street beef with Five and Sunny's crew. He used to pillow talk with Lauren every night because he thought she truly understood him and the lifestyle. But little did Sean P know she was soaking it all up to use it against him.

Lauren never told her baby father she went to school with Sunny and that they used to talk once upon a time. Yesterday, she inboxed him on Facebook and requested to meet up and he sent a location a few blocks away from where she lived. Lauren left her baby with her mom for a few days until she could gain strength. Lauren was an emotional wreck right now. She couldn't even drive correctly. She felt like Sean P broke her soul. The two were supposed to get married in three months.

***

Sunny waited in front of his car in front of a gated oil company surrounded by towers and warehouses. It was 10 p.m. and he wanted to spend some time with Rachel. Sunny had been so busy trying to lay low and focus on a bag because the city was turning up. Now that Five was gone, Sunny knew he would be next on the law enforcement's hit list. He felt like letting Rags run the show was brilliant because he was still fresh out and nobody really knew who he was as of yet.

Seeing Lauren inbox him, he couldn't help but assume she wanted some dick because she missed her chance back in high school. Sunny loved Rachel, but he was still a man, and cheating was just a part of life. He figured as long as he kept it respectful and his dirt didn't get back to Rachel, it was okay. Lauren was looking good on social media even after a baby, and she had lips made for dick sucking, so he couldn't wait to test drive her.

Lauren pulled up almost hitting his tail lights. He looked at her like she was bugging. When she got out Lauren thighs was busting out her jeans.

"Hey Sunny," Lauren said, fixing her wild hair.

"How you been, Lauren? You look good." Sunny could tell something was on her mind and it wasn't sex.

"Thanks. I need to talk you."

"That's why I'm here."

"You know Sean P?" she asked, seeing him give her an awkward look.

"Maybe. Why?"

"Listen, I know about y'all beef, and he's trying to kill you. His boss, X, is the one who killed Five, and I heard he was related to you. He lives in PG county in a mini mansion. It's real nice. Sean P's little sister Pearla just came back from college in D.C. She is a correctional officer now at the county jail." Lauren was talking so fast she had to take a break to breathe.

"Why the fuck are you telling me all of this?" he asked suspiciously.

"Sean P violated me and I want him dead."

"Okay. I see." Sunny hated bitches like Lauren because they would flip at any given moment, even after you gave them the world. This is why he trusted nobody.

"Do you need more info?"

"Nah, Lauren, you done given me more than enough" Sunny smoothly pulled out a 9mm handgun and aimed it at her forehead.

Sunny killed Lauren because he knew if anything would happen to Sean P, she would most likely switch and turn on him.

***

Downtown, B-more

Hours later

Rags called Sunny and came to his condo, which was some upscale shit. Rags had to check in at the lobby area before the guards let him in the elevator. The mayor of the city even lived in the complex.

Rags was all done with the product Baby Blood and Kanno were down to 500 grams or less until Sunny made another trip to New York.

Sunny's apartment door was cracked open so he walked inside to see Sunny placing one finger over his lips, telling him to come on. Sunny took Rags to his office, which was soundproof. Rachel was asleep in the master bedroom and he didn't want her to hear their conversation.

"Why you call me so late?" Sunny asked, yawning.

"I need more dog food. What else I'ma call you for?"

"I gotta make a trip."

"When? Because niggas ain't got shit, bro, facts. I collected all the money so everything is in place," Rags said.

"Sometime this week. But I've been meaning to hit you anyway"

"Shit, you got my number."

"I spoke to Sean P's girlfriend or whoever that bitch was and she gave me the drop on him."

"Damn, that easy? Are you sure its official?" Rags knew how dirty chicks could be.

"It was all valid, little bro. We got the full drop on him and dude's family," said Sunny, smiling.

"A'ight, bet, let's make it happen."

"Nah, we gonna wait for a second. Let's focus on this paper."

"I'm saying, we got him right where we want him. Why not make our move?"

"Sometime when we don't have patience, bad things come."

"Let me find out you getting soft, my nigga. Hit me whenever you ready," Rags said, leaving.

Chapter 29
North, Baltimore

Dozen easily unlocked the lobby door and rushed the building with his crime buddies Longhead and Haper. The apartment on the first floor was a known drug trafficking apartment, which one of Dozen's snitches put him on to.

"Don't forget, in and out. We got less than three minutes, starting now," Dozen said, kicking in the door with no warning.

"Oh my God!" a thick redbone chick screamed, jumping up from sucking two niggas' dicks at a time.

Everybody froze naked in the living room.

"Look at them boobs on her," Longhead said, staring at the redbone's DD titties.

"Where is the money and drugs?" Dozen asked.

"You got the wrong crib, and it's clear y'all don't know who you niggas fucking with," the tall dark one said, using a pillow to cover his privates.

Dozen laughed and looked at him.

Boc! Boc! Boc! Boc!

Bullets violently smashed into the tall dude's chest as his body crashed within seconds.

"Do I have to ask again?" Dozen looked at the redbone and the short chubby nigga.

"Living room closet," the woman said, fearing for her life.

"Thank you."

Haper and Longhead went to the closet to snatch the bag they saw.

Dozen was watching the two victims to make sure they didn't run or try anything dumb.

"You that dirty cop," the short guy said.

"Why don't you just shut the fuck up before I shut you up, fat ass," Dozen said before he heard gunshot.

"Fuck!" Haper yelled.

"What happened back there?" asked Dozen seeing Longhead coming out with a saddened look.

"He shot a kid," Longhead stated, and the redbone woman started yelling and screaming for her six-year-old son.

"How the fuck——" Dozen said seeing the short nigga jump for his gun on the chair.

Boc!

Boc!

Boc!

Boc!

Boc!

Boc!

Longhead and Dozen lit his ass up with bullets, killing him on the couch, then training their gun on the redbone woman, emptying the clips.

Haper came out with tears and the money and drugs, which was only five kilos and ten stacks.

"We gotta go. Don't call it in and put your mask on," Dozen said, seeing Haper was zoned out. "Haper, come on, get it together, brother," Dozen said before leading the way back outside.

The whole ride back to their secret location, Haper didn't say a word while Dozen and Longhead talked about another lick in mind. Haper had two little boys himself, so killing kids he was against, even though the little boy startled him coming out of his room. Haper thought the kid was a gunman, so he fired and killed the kid. Haper felt sad and worthless. He didn't want this type of lifestyle as a cop.

***

Hazelton, West VA

The Hazelton Women's Federal Prison visitation room was almost empty today as Fatima sat there playing with her red manicured nails. She been waiting for only ten minutes, but it felt like an hour.

Fatima hadn't seen her mom in about two years because she was trying to finish up school and become a cop. Her mom was her biggest supporter. Proof was also, even though at first, he frowned upon her wishes to become a cop in Baltimore. Proof suggested she become a cop in Philly, D.C. or New Jersey, but she loved B-more.

ReRe came out in her prison uniform, looking healthy and young, as if she could pass for Fatima's sister instead of her mother.

"Look at my baby." ReRe hugged her daughter so tightly that the C.O. had to look and make sure Fatima was still alive.

"Thanks for the pictures."

"No problem, baby. How's work? I'm so proud of you." ReRe couldn't stop smiling. Seeing her daughter break the family curse was a blessing. Even though ReRe never sold drugs, she did help Proof invest drug money into businesses and stocks. She was the brains to his operations. The DA called her a mastermind at sentencing in court.

"I love it, but a lot of crazy things are going on."

"Oh, that's life. You just gotta protect yourself and stay safe. Have you spoken to your brother?"

"No, not really," Fatima said sadly.

"You kids used to be so close. That's the only family you have. I know they do wrong, and you can't risk your career, but don't disown them. The Scott family never turns our back on each other."

"Yes, Mommy." Fatima knew her mom was right.

"I want you to do the right thing in life: go to school, find a boyfriend."

"I be so busy, OMG!"

Fatima talked and laughed with her mom until the visit was over.

Chapter 30
Westside, B-more

HD moved his car dealership to a new and improved location, which had more traffic, surprisingly, then the old downtown establishment. When Jack got killed, he knew the police would shut the place down because of the lease and insurance, which he put in Jack's name for safety reasons.

Sean P arrived out front. Not wanting his employees to hear his conversation, he stepped out of the dealership.

"Antoine, I will be right back," HD said, fixing his shirt collar before looking at his Rolex watch.

"Okay, boss" the new intern stated, doing paperwork.

"New spot, I see," Sean P said, looking around the lot, which was filled with all types of cars. Sean P always copped his cars from HD because he only had a 400 four hundred credit score and no other dealership was going for that shit.

"Yeah, I had to after what happened to Jack."

"They just killed my baby mother," Sean P said sadly. He spent three days in a room trying to clear his head and make sense of who could have done this horrible crime. Deep down, he knew who, but didn't want to yet admit it to himself.

"That's crazy. Sorry to hear that. Is your son okay?"

"Yeah. He's with her mom, tucked away and safe." Sean P knew it was his fault Lauren was dead, but he would not let it keep him down. He would get back.

"Good, because now it's time to take something they love, slim," said HD in deep thought.

"You got a plan?"

"One of them little niggas' moms used to be my taste tester, but she be in the Southside of town now."

"Which one?"

"Kanno." HD hoped he got the young man's name right.

"I want that Sunny kid."

"That makes both of us, Sean, but patience is a must."

"If your child's mother was just killed, would you still be saying that?"

"To be truthful, slim, I don't know what I would do because I hate my children's mothers, so they would have did me a favor," HD said, making Sean P laugh.

"I feel that."

"I'ma have that info on Kanno's mom, but I 've been meaning to speak with you anyway. Walk with me," HD said. He saw customers walking around looking at cars, so he walked through the lot.

"What's up? Is it about the re-up?" Sean P still had the money at his house for the next shipment, but the death of his baby mother had him on standstill.

"Nah. I'll have someone pick it up whenever you ready. But you hear what happened to LB?"

"Yeah. Someone did him dirty"

"I been hearing Polo and his crew is beefing with Baby Blood and Kanno." HD had been hearing a lot of street gossip about the two allies.

"I can ask around, because somebody is supplying them niggas better product then Five used to have."

"Sunny may have found a new plug. I don't know, but we starting to lose money and good men."

"This team-up with X I don't really agree with. We don't need him." Sean P didn't really like X. He felt like the man was too smart for himself.

"No worries. I got X, young'un. One thing about life: some people come into your life for a reason, and it's on you how to use them," HD said.

"If you say so."

"Go home, clear your head, spend some time with your son, and come back in full force, slim."

"A'ight." Sean P walked off.

HD called out to him. "Sean! I need you to get focused, because a storm is coming, and I need you to be on float."

HD saw Sean P nod his head, approving the concerns, but he was more than ready.

***

East, B-more

Baby Blood and over twenty young thugs posted up in the park, ready to kill for the late C Bloody. Last night, Sha and two of his goons caught C Bloody coming out of a club and killed him. Two more Piru members were shot in the shootout, but their injuries weren't life threatening at all.

"Tonight, we gonna shake the city and hit every block belonging to Polo and Sha". Baby Blood looked at his crew, all flossing red flags.

Everybody was quiet, thinking about the good times they all had with C Bloody, who was the funniest nigga in the crew with a big heart.

"Show no mercy on these bitch-ass niggas," Baby Blood stated, looking at the four SUVs ready to spin Sha's and Polo's blocks until everybody outside was a target getting hit. The whole gang filled up the trucks and went hunting.

Chapter 31
Downtown, B-more

Haper walked into the police station where he worked after a week off on vacation. Since killing the kid in the house raid, Haper's mind had been fucked up. The sight of the little boy haunted his thoughts and dreams. He had been ducking Longhead's and Dozen's calls since the incident took place because he couldn't get down with them no more. That was the straw that broke the camel's back.

"Boss, you busy?" Haper went into Captain White's office.

"Come in, Detective."

"Looks different in here. I like what you've done with the place," Haper said before taking a seat.

"You haven't been in here since only God knows when. But how can I help you, Detective? Dozen says you doing a great job out there."

Hearing the name "Dozen" sent chills up Haper's spine as he thought about the recent event.

"Detective, you okay?" Captain White saw Haper was zoned out for a minute.

"Oh, yeah. I came to ask if I can take some time off? I got a lot going on right now."

"Is everything okay?" His boss seemed very concerned.

"I'm okay, just dealing with a lot of family issues."

"Haper, you're a good cop, so take as long as you need and I'll make sure you still get paid."

"Thanks, Cap. I'll be back, but I have to get my shit together," Haper said as he stood up to leave.

"Haper, are you sure there is nothing you want to talk about? Because you look a little off."

"I'm good, boss, thanks for asking." Haper walked out of his captain's office and down the hall, hearing someone call his name, but he ignored them. When he stopped at the elevator, he saw that Dozen and Longhead had caught up to him.

"We was calling you," Longhead said, out of breath.

"Oh , my bad, I didn't even hear you guys."

"You was speaking to Captain White?" said Dozen, giving off a funny look.

"Yeah. I told him I need a break."

"A break? For what?" Longhead looked confused.

"Got a lot going on."

"You not thinking about breaking our friendship off, are you?" Dozen questioned

"No, Dozen, I just need some time to clear my head," Haper explained.

"Fair."

"Haper, we need you, buddy." Longhead placed his arm around Haper's shoulders.

"I'm just exhausted."

Haper saw Dozen give him the cold stare. "Let him go. We understand, Haper. Get yourself together," Dozen said as the elevator opened.

"Thanks for understanding," Haper said, rushing into the elevator with his head down as Dozen and Longhead both watched him closely.

***

Brooklyn, NY

Sunny came out to downtown BK so he could meet with the plug who requested for Sunny to bring Rags along this time. Sunny had no problem doing that but Sunny liked handling business operations one on one - the less people the better.

"Where dude at, yo?" Rags said, impatient because he wanted to get the dope and get back to the bag.

"Relax, bro. He'll be here, ugly little nigga. Fatima went to see Mommy," Sunny said, reading a book in a local library.

"About time."

"Don't do that, shawty. Our sister trying to make a better way of living for us."

"Or herself."

"Cut it out, bro. Fatima loves us. She made the right choice," Sunny said, seeing North and an older gentleman walk into the library, heading their way.

"That's them?" asked Rags.

"Gentlemen, sorry for the lateness, but this is my father, Abdullah. He runs the family and show," North said as his dad looked at both men with a stern look before saying anything.

"So you two are my brother's boys?" the dark skin African man said in a deep voice.

"Yes. Good to meet you, Uncle," Sunny said.

"I ain't know we was African," Rags tried to whisper, but everybody overheard him.

"Yes, young Doug, your blood roots are from the motherland. Not this American shit. I came to the States very young with my parents, Proof, Five, and a few of my other young brothers were born over here, which is a sad thing. We still have a lot of family back in Africa," Abdullah said.

"Damn. I would have never known, but Daddy did mention this a few times," Rags said.

"I'm sure he did. I just wanted to meet my nephews. I have to go now, but we will meet again" Abdullah got up and left.

North and the men spoke about the money and car sitting outside waiting with the drugs inside as well as a lady driver ready to follow them back to B-more.

Chapter 32
Eastside, B-more

Twenty-four hours later, Rags, Baby Blood, and Kanno met up at Lafayette, a well-known drug section Baby Blood now controlled. In the last two days, eight from Baby Blood's and Sha's side were murdered cold-bloodedly.

The gun violence was getting crazy. Two of Sha's men got killed in a school zone this morning, leaving a teacher also shot dead on the scene. The police ended up arresting three of Baby Blood's soldiers on the murders hours ago.

Rags opened the trash bag full of keys. There were forty inside and the rest he put up because he was running out of product before it was time to see the plug, which was bad business.

"This the same shit as last time, right?" asked Baby Blood.

"Why wouldn't it be, shawty?" Rags smiled, looking at Kanno, who was sitting down on his iPhone acting anti-social.

"Niggas been spinning on Sha's and Polo's blocks day and night. The city on fire right now. Police running down on dealers and fiends, bro." Baby Blood shook his head, disappointed.

"Let shit cool down for a day or two and drop off money to any fallen soldiers' family members," said Rags.

"That's already said and done." Baby Blood loved his homies and would always keep their honor and oath alive.

"You good, Kanno?" Rags knew when something was on his boy's mind. He had been around him too long.

"Yeah. I was texting Fat P. He's on his way into town from Philly." Kanno didn't even look at Baby Blood. Being around him upset his stomach.

"What about that case?" asked Rags.

"I believe he good, bro. I'ma make some calls." Rags planned to speak to Dozen again to make sure Fat P was good, but the last time they spoke, he said Fat P was in the clear.

"A'ight." Rags handed each man twenty kilos, then checked his new Rolex for the time because he had a meeting with a broker and realtor about another house he saw next to his apartment. Rags had already bought one home and he hoped today the realtor could bring down the price. Rags' plan was to buy as many homes as he could, fix them up, and re-sell them for triple the price he bought them for. The real estate business was safe, smart, and very profitable on his end, so this is what he really planned to do when he retired from the game in a few years.

***

North Village, B-more

Jena waited for her client outside of the nice home with a small two car garage connected to the side of the home. Four bedrooms, four bathrooms, a game room, magnificent kitchen, and it was a two-level home.

In her mid-thirties, Jena had her life in order as well as the perfect curvy body she spent endless hours in the gym working on. Her cocoa brown skin, neatly-done dreads, and perfect million-dollar smile did something to almost every male that passed her, plus her soft eyes screamed "fuck me. But Jena's sexual side was only for one man, and that was X. He showed Jena how to get money, save, and become successful in life.

X taught Jena so much over the few years and catered to her with so much love that she had no choice but to marry the man she fell in love with. She knew marriage wasn't all peaches and cream because there were times she caught X cheating. Jena's mom always taught her that a man will always be a man, even when they go to the grave. Her love for X she knew would never come again, so she stuck around.

A white Maybach 600 pulled up behind her SUV. She wondered if it was her client. If so, Jena assumed he was a rich white man with style. When Jena saw a very handsome young black man climb out of the driver's seat in a black designer suit, she was more than amazed.

"Hey, I'm Doug. We briefly spoke over the phone." Rags extended his hand, a little caught off guard by her beauty.

"Nice to meet you. I'm...umm..." Jena laughed at herself for almost forgetting her own name.

"This is a beautiful home. When I saw it, there was no way I could go by without stopping," Rags stated, looking at the perfectly-shaped bricks.

"It's one of my favorites, to be honest, and this area is quiet."

"I live nearby."

"Oh wow, that's great! If you don't mind me asking, what do you do for a living?" she asked, smelling his Fendi cologne for men.

"I'm a real estate agent," Rags proudly told her, already knowing she was thinking the worst.

"Okay, so you must be going to re-sell the place, I assume."

"Yes. This is why I would like a better retail price on it, but I'm not trying to cut into your profit," he explained.

"Understood. We can talk about it. Let me give you a tour," Jena stated, turning to go inside, giving Rags a full look at her nice, round ass.

Chapter 33
North, B-more

Haper got out of the shower drying, himself off while his wife cooked dinner for him and the kids. Since leaving work, he had been attending counseling to get off the nightmares of the little boy he had shot and killed on his last mission with Dozen.

Spending time at home with the kids somewhat brought him back to reality of life. He didn't give two damns about how Dozen or Longhead thought about him breaking off because unlike them, Haper had a family to look after.

Once dressed, he went downstairs to smell something over-cooking in the oven. "Robin, is something burning?" he yelled to his wife, touching the last step, then everything happened so fast.

A metal object crashed into his forehead, knocking him to the floor, making it hard to see, but the voice he had heard one too many times was clear.

"I missed you, Haper, buddy." Longhead dragged his body into the living room to join his family, who were on the living room couch crying. The sight of his two little boys and his wife crying brought tears to Haper eyes.

Dozen stood over his family with two guns out, smiling.

"I hate it has to come to this, my black brother, but you leave me no choice, Haper." Dozen shook his head and took a deep breath.

"You're going to hell for this. Both of you!" Haper screamed.

"Not before you, baby killer. Don't you remember the little kid you just killed? Or did it exit your mind already. Cold-hearted motherfucker."

"That's why I liked him," Longhead said as if he was already dead.

"Nice, Haper, just fucking nice. You're killing kids?" Robin said, upset and fearful.

"Baby, it was a mistake."

Haper's own kids were now more scared of him than the killer who they saw come by daily. Robin let the two cops inside because she thought they came to check on her husband until they pointed a loaded gun at her.

"We gotta go, Dozen," said Longhead.

"Farewell, Haper."

Dozen and Longhead killed everybody in the house before lighting it on fire. Within twenty minutes, the lifeless bodies were all burned to crisps by the time police, ambulance, and the fire department got there.

***

North Village, B-more

Carena woke up, looking around the posh room to see a fresh rose on the dresser next to her head. She couldn't believe what took place last night, but to say she regretted it would be a big lie. She went out to the movies last night, then came back to Rags' place for dinner he made, which was good. The two started drinking wine and Carena made the first move because she was horny and hadn't been touched by a man in a long time. Things led to the bedroom, where they made love for hours, very passionate sex. She even heard him slip up and say he loved her, but Carena knew her pussy was fire and would cause a nigga to say anything.

Carena had to rush home to get ready for work, but she did wonder where he would go at 8 a.m. She was not trying to be nosy, but she couldn't help it and started going through his things.

Seeing his Maybach last night for the first time made her wonder if people could really make money like that doing real estate, but she figured he had some money left over from when he went to jail.

Searching through his drawers, closets, and hallway closets, Carena saw nothing except blueprints of homes he was re-building, so she felt bad, but there was still a little doubt. Looking around, she had to admit he had a nice, classy, and fancy taste, just like her.

Carena took a shower, left him a note, and went home to get dressed, thinking about last night, which made her smile all day.

***

Downtown, B-more

Fatima sat across from her brother Sunny, trying to find the right words to say because she was at a loss for them.

"You look great." Sunny broke the very long, awkward silence.

"Thanks. Hard work, I guess," Fatima said, nibbling around the pancakes she ordered from a known diner.

"Mommy said you went to visit?"

"Yeah. I'ma go see Daddy next month. Maybe you should come"

"I don't know. I'm trying stay away from the federal thing," Sunny said.

"That's hard to tell," she shot back with a neck roll.

"Fatima, you know this curse is hard to break. You think there aren't times I want to just move away and open a chain of legit businesses?"

"Why don't you, Sunny? What more could you ask for really?" She saw him pause and knew she had caught him.

"There are some things you wouldn't understand, sis."

"Well, help me, because from how I see it, people are out here dying over drugs every day. You are destroying us black people as a whole, so don't turn a wrong into a right. Selling drugs and killing people is an option, Sunny. If you're not part of the solution, you are the problem." Fatima looked him dead in his eyes, seeing she had hit a spot.

"You're right, baby sister." Sunny knew Fatima spoke the truth.

"I know." She smiled

"You run into Dozen yet?"

Fatima's smile faded upon hearing Dozen's name. "No, and I don't plan to."

"Why do you dislike Uncle Dozen so much?" Sunny always wondered.

"Just don't like him; that's all."

"Fatima, you just can't hate nobody for no reason."

"Well, I do, and I have to get back to work." Fatima ended that topic by getting up to leave in her work uniform under her raincoat because today was a rainy, nasty day.

"You don't have to."

"I feel you, but you don't always have to be tough. Some people like myself aren't afraid of that police badge of yours." Sunny smiled.

"Well, you should," she joked as they walked outside, talking and laughing like how they used to do as kids.

Outside, a smoke gray Cadillac circle the parking lot as Sunny walked Fatima to her car. Sunny looked to his left and saw HD's arm extending out the window with a gun while Sean P drove, grinning. Shit was in slow motion, but Fatima got a quick glance at the men as Sunny tackled her to the wet ground.

Bloc! Bloc! Bloc! Bloc! Bloc! Bloc!

The Cadillac spun off after hitting Sunny six times in his back while he was covering Fatima. She screamed, in tears, rushing to call 911 as her brother said the word "family" before dying in her arms.

People came outside to help as the police rushed the lot a minute later, but Sunny was already gone.

Chapter 34
Fella Point, B-more

Rags dropped what he was doing to rush to Fatima. She had called him, crying and screaming that Sunny died. Rags couldn't believe it and was on his way to her, Kanno called and said the same thing. Everything was spinning in his head as they pulled into a nice complex area.

Fatima was outside sitting on a bench in her work uniform with bloodstains all over. Rags jumped out of the Maybach, almost forgetting to put it in park.

"What happened?" he said as she lifted her head and jumped in his arms, crying like a baby.

Rags didn't even need to ask again what happened. Fatima's actions spoke for itself.

"It's gonna be okay," he said, holding his sister, trying to keep his emotions intact, but losing Sunny was a big loss.

"No, it's not. They just killed him"

"Who?"

"I don't know. We were coming out of the diner and I saw a car pull up with two people inside, then it all happened so fast. Sunny died trying to protect me," she said, crying on his chest again.

"Listen, this is not your fight, Fatima. We chose this lifestyle."

"We? I thought you was doing real estate."

"Fatima, this is in my blood and you know it."

"Look what just happened to Five and Sunny. Our bloodline is disappearing because we not trying to change it. Mommy and Daddy never coming home. Doug, open your eyes. You all I have left out here."

"I know, and I'm not going nowhere, trust me." Rags understood where she was coming from, but he had to carry the family torch now alone.

"When the police called, I couldn't even ID Sunny because the station don't know I'm related to y'all. I had to call Rachel down, then I took the day off."

"Do you remember who pulled the trigger or who was driving?" he asked.

"They was in a smoke gray Cadillac. I have the license plate in my head already. I didn't give it to nobody, but I want blood, not prison for them." The real Scott came out of Fatima.

"Spoken like a true Scott."

"Just clean up your fucking tracks, Doug, please," she begged.

"Always. But did you see the shooter?"

"He was an older fat guy with a beard, and the driver was a handsome brown-skinned dude. I couldn't really get a good look at the driver because of the tinted window," she explained.

"Okay, I'ma look into it."

"I will too. But Doug, this life can't last forever."

"Maybe not, but for now, I'ma make the best outta it and put on for our family. We big steppers. These niggas crawling," Rags said, making her crack a smile at his dumb comment.

"I love you." She gave him a tight hug.

"Love you too."

***

President Street, B-more

Sean P checked his AP bust down, waiting for officer MacDile to arrive next to a shopping center. Yesterday was a big day for him. Seeing Sunny's body get riddled with bullets made Sean feel as if he was on top again.

It was hard for him to see who the female was with Sunny, but whoever the pretty chick was, Sunny saved her life. At first, he and HD were on their way to HD's car dealership when they spotted Sunny's milky white Audi coupe parked in the diner lot. When they peeped Sunny coming out, HD took Sean P's pistol to show him how it was supposed to be done. Now that the Scott family was out of the picture, they could take over the city. The Scott family had a lot of turf, but Sean P had a few ideas to get the rest of the Scott family workers to turn sides and come work for him and HD.

A Dodge truck pulled up and Sean P got out his car to speak with the newest law enforcement on their team, Officer MacDile Longhead.

"Sean P. Word is you the one who took Sunny out," Longhead joked

"I never heard of him. But good to see you, cracker. What made you come to our side?"

"The pay. And speaking of pay…my money please, sir." Longhead extended his hand as Sean P smirked and placed a folder inside it.

"Now talk. What information you have for us?"

"Well, first off, Dozen been the one who robbed two of your spots."

"I knew it was that bitch-ass nigga," Sean spat.

"Then to make shit worse, a new federal DA named Carena is building a case on you and Baby Blood, so if I was you, Sean P, I's get the fuck outta town or take care of her. Meet me here next Sunday, same time and same pay." Longhead got back in his truck, peeling off.

Sean P climbed in his car, trying to let it all soak in, unaware a car parked across the street had been watching him since he arrived.

Chapter 35
Cherry Hill, B-more

Kanno came out to the classy middle-class neighborhood to meet up with a crazy ex-girlfriend who had been blowing up his phone, talking about a baby and child support fees. Since dealing with Pearla, he had been giving any free time he had to her because she was dope and really worth it.

Parking in front of a big house, he texted Ashley, telling her to come outside. When Kanno saw how big Ashley's stomach was, he wanted to pull off on her.

"What the fuck is that?" Kanno asked her when she climbed in the passenger seat like a fat bitch.

"I'm pregnant with your child, dummy, what it look like?" she yelled.

"Calm down. Maybe this is some type of mistake because when I was dealing with you, Ashley, you came clean eventually and said you had a boyfriend named Chewy."

"Eventually after we fucked raw, yes, but Chewy is dead now Kanno." She got a little sad thinking about the love of her life, Chewy. She loved Chewy, but his dick was small, so Ashley went to other guys to pleasure her. But the love she had for him, couldn't no man ever hold.

"Well, RIP to dude. I guess he left a seed behind."

"Kanno, this is not funny. This is either yours or Sha's baby, and somebody about to take a DNA and pay child support" She continued to talk, but Kanno's mind was stuck on hearing Sha's name.

"Sha?"

"Yes. He nutted all up in me too, the same day as you. Don't judge me; you niggas are nasty. At least I can find you. I can't get in touch with that bitch made nigga." She got heated.

"Calm down, sexy, we gonna figure it out," Kanno sweet talked her, grabbing her chin.

"I can't raise a kid alone. My mom and dad are ready to put me out, I don't have a job, and I got two STD's. My life sucks," she cried.

"STD's?" Kanno couldn't believe this crazy bitch

"Yes, but I'ma go get the cream for it tomorrow. Some nigga last week gave it to me"

"Damn, you pregnant, Ashley, slow down. You don't want your baby to come out fucked up"

"You're a dick." She laughed.

"This Sha dude…where he from? Maybe I can see if someone knows him?" Kanno rubbed her inner thigh, knowing how freaky she was.

"Southside of that ghetto place I used to hate going to. His apartment over there. I swear, if it wasn't for the dick---"

"I ain't trying to hear all that."

"My bad; just being honest. But yours is hitting all the right spots too." She rubbed his manhood through his jeans as it came to life.

"What block was it?"

"Where Sha lives on?" she asked, still stroking his penis, licking her lips.

"Yes."

"Bank Street, next to that store they all be at. But fuck him. I want this." She pulled out his hardened rod and placed it on her lips.

Ashley started sucking the tip in a slow motion. Kanno wanted to stop her, but the shit felt so good, he let her do her thing.

She lowered her head down deeper, taking him into the back of her throat before raising up. Ashley bopped up and down, switching her speed from fast to slow making him grab the door panel. When he nutted, Ashley caught every drop with a smile.

"Damn."

"Come see me later. I want you to feel this wet pussy."

"Maybe next time." Kanno just remembered about her two STD's and thought against it before kicking her out of his car.

Chapter 36
Downtown B-more

Carena been working late all week, trying to put together the Baby Blood case and Sean P's caseload. Both men were accused of at least half a dozen murders in the city. She pulled up both of their files and they had rap sheets longer than T.I.'s. Seeing all the crazy shit these two crews were being charged with was a real insult to what she was seeing with her own eyes. The crimes stemmed back to five years ago when Proof the kingpin had a lock on the city. The files said Sean P worked for an unknown dealer and Baby Blood's file stated he was second in command under Five, dealing with the Piru gang.

Carena's eyes burned from reading paperwork all day. It was 10:05 p.m. The building closed at 8 p.m., but she had a lot of extra work to do, so Carena stayed a little late. But now it was time to go.

She grabbed her Louis Vuitton bag and headed downstairs. There were two security guards in the lobby there at all times 24/7.

"Have a good night, gentlemen," she said to the two fat black guards watching the *Snowfall* TV show on their phone.

"You too." Both guards looked at the way her ass jiggled in her slacks as they wondered how good she looked with her clothes off.

The parking lot only had a few cars outside as Carena walked to her BMW. A truck crept up from out of a parking spot and ran into her from behind, knocking her face first into the ground. Two men rushed out of the truck as if they were there to help.

"You looked into the wrong can of worms, bitch," Sean P said, grabbing Carena by her hair while the 6'6" tall big man lifted her ankles, trying to drag her into the truck. Sean P had plans to let his goons rape her then kill her, leaving no type of trace. Since Longhead informed him of what was going on, he had to do something to save his ass.

"Help!" she screamed

"Bitch, shut up!" Sean P punched her in the mouth, almost getting Carena inside the backseat until everything went wrong.

Bloc, Bloc, Bloc, Bloc, Bloc, Bloc, Bloc!

Sean P soldier's upper torso got hit with bullets, dropping him, and he let Carena feet free. She kicked Sean P in his nuts, then took off running.

Bloc, Bloc, Bloc!

A bullet hit Sean P in his arm, making him climb into the truck to get outta sight because his gun was under the seat, but unfortunately, the shooter had the drop on him. Before swerving out of the lot, Sean P got a good look at the gunman. It was Rags.

***

Rags caught up with Carena and calmed her down. She was panicking, scared, and lost.

"We have to go. Come on." Rags put her in his getaway car with force because at first, she didn't want to go.

Once far away from the scene, she calmed down a little, but was still shaken up somewhat.

"You just killed someone," was all she could say.

"They were about to kill you, Carena. Why would they come for you?" Rags questioned because he had been tailing Sean P all day and when he saw him come to Carena's job, he figured Sean P had intentions to get info outta her or kill her to send a memo.

"I don't know," she lied.

"You know something, and right now isn't the right time to hold shit back," he warned her.

"Okay, I'm building a case on Sean P and a kid named Baby Blood, but I don't know. How did they know so fast?" She was more confused than anything.

"Baby Blood?"

"Yes, you heard of him? Maybe he had something to do with this too," she assumed.

"Trust me, Baby Blood had nothing to do with this."

"How the hell you know, Doug?"

"Because that's my people, and I need you to drop that case or it can link back to me." He spoke the truth even if it hurt her to hear he was back on bullshit.

"I got people trying to kill me and now I find out you know these people. What is really going on, Doug? I feel like you're not being 100% truthful."

"Carena, you're no dummy. I'm pretty sure you can do the math."

"You lied to me." She shook her head, disappointed.

"No, I hid something from you because I love you."

The words "I love you" caught her by a big surprise. She paused and had to let it soak in.

"Where are you taking me?"

"Somewhere safe for the night," he said, driving to the outskirts of Baltimore to a new home he had just purchased yesterday and planned to flip.

"I just wanna sleep."

"You will." Rags couldn't believe Sean P just tried a bold move like that, but he couldn't blame him.

Chapter 36
Eastside, B-more

Polo and Sha were shooting a little hoop this morning outside to get some fresh air. Ten goons surrounded the gate entrance with guns just in case something popped off.

"Nice tan," Sha told Polo, who was hitting 96 percent of his 3-point shots. Since he was a kid, he had dreams of going to the NBA or at least overseas, but the streets had other plans for Polo.

"You know how that Miami life is, bro," Polo replied fresh back from a two-week trip there.

"I find it crazy how when shit gets thick, you make it for a vacation. We out here losing men, blocks, and money," Sha said, speaking his mind because since the whole shit popped off, he had been front line and Polo had been hiding. Even LB was starting to lose respect for Polo, his own brother, before he got killed.

"Sha, I'm not a killer. I never been that or acted as if I was that. I'm a drug dealer and businessman," Polo made clear.

"I understand, but this is your fight too. Them niggas killed my brother years ago and now they murdered yours."

"Sha, my brother knew what came with this shit just like we both do. Sunny and Five is dead. It's not hard to wipe out a bunch of little niggas." Polo stopped shooting ball and got serious.

"These niggas got the most numbers in the city from the east, south, and southeast section they got on lock, bro," Sha replied.

"I pay you to run this shit, Sha, and it's looking like I put my trust in the wrong person."

"Polo, I gave this my blood, sweat, and tears. What can you say?"

"Don't disrespect me. I feed all of you niggas out here!" Polo yelled.

"Sometimes it's not about the money, shawty. It's about the honor we live by," Sha said before walking off, leaving Polo on the court alone to think.

***

USP Victorville, Cali

The last week, the jail had been on lockdown because two different states crashed on the yard. Twelve people were outside stabbing each other over a prison TV none of them would be seeing no time soon in the box.

Hearing the news about Sunny a few days ago crushed Proof to hear his older son dead. Two losses back to back was too much to handle in prison with no release date because a person had to hold those emotions in or else people would feed off that.

A C.O. popped up at his window with a new inmate fresh off the bus.

"Mr. Scott, you're getting a celly. I'll bring the mattress up in a few," Correctional Officer Roseadle, a racist old white man who had been at the jail twenty years, stated.

Proof saw the young man step in his cell with a bed roll and a Baltimore number on his shirt. Proof moved his prayer rug off the floor and books off the top bunk for the young man, who looked a little familiar.

"What's up, home team. You from the city of Baltimore?" Proof asked

"Yeah. I'm from southeast," the young brother said, sitting on a chair.

"Southeast? Shit, that's my old area young'un, who you related to?" Proof ain't run into too many people from his side of town; mainly the west and east.

"Rain is my mom."

"Hold the fuck up, yo, your name is Nice? Little Kanno's older brother?" Proof knew Rain had three kids and one was somewhere in the feds doing life for a murder.

"Yeah, that's me. You must be Proof. Everybody be talking about you. I remember you from when I was little." Nice smiled, thinking about the old days.

"Damn, shawty, it's been a while. Where you coming from?" asked Proof.

"Coleman USP in Florida."

"I heard that's a sweet joint," Proof stated.

"Somewhat. We had a big race riot down there. You know how them racist white boys get. So one of the D.C. homies stabbed the shit outta the biggest one and shit went up. That bitch still on lock-down, yo," said Nice with two war wounds on his chest to prove it.

"Damn, young'un. You ever get back in court yet?"

"They denied my 2255 motion, so now I'm just waiting on some new laws to drop, yo."

"Same shit here. Just waiting."

"I heard about Sunny and Five. That shit touched my heart. You got my regards," Nice said. He and Sunny used to be best of friends.

"That street life ain't worth it, but it's in my family DNA. I really wish it wasn't young'un"

"I heard Rags and my little brother out there playing hard ball." Nice had been hearing a lot of stories about the two.

"As a father, I can only give good advice and pray to Allah for his safety."

"Facts."

Nice and Proof talked and made a meal with the sink's hot water.

Chapter 37
Southside, B-more

Honey and Rain were both on their way to a dope house for their morning fix, something they had to have every wake up. Honey was a pretty slim young chick who let heroin fuck up her life two years ago while in college. After her mother died, Honey started to deal with many drugs, but dog food had always been her go-to drug.

Rain was another story. She lived for getting high over twenty years on dope, crack, and coke, whatever she could get her dirty hands on. All her kids was basically grown except Egypt, but this was about to be her first year of college. Nice was locked up doing a life bid in prison and Kanno ran the streets doing God knows what. Last week she saw Kanno driving a luxury car and made him give her $200 dollars in back rent.

"Stop walking so slow," Rain said with her fast-paced walk.

"You walk too fast, Rain."

"This a nice car," Rain said, looking at a big body BMW parked in front of the trap house where some young'uns sold dope for the low. But it wasn't fucking with that eastside shit Baby Blood had.

"Wild, we got money today," Rain said through the boarded-up window on the side of the house.

"Man, how much? Because last time you two bitches said the same shit and lied," Wild said.

"But we made up for it and sucked five of y'all nasty dicks," Honey said, rolling her beautiful eyes that always tricked niggas. If Honey didn't wear dirty fiend clothes, nobody would ever think she did hard drugs.

"And we swallowed," Rain added.

"Okay, come in through the back." Wild went to let them in thinking about how good their oral sex was last time.

Once inside, they followed Wild to a back room, stepping over fiends who looked dead, but they were just high and enjoying the trip.

"I never been back here. We get special treatment today," Honey said as they walked into a dimmed room to see a husky guy.

"HD," said Rain.

"It's been a long time," HD said, now coming towards them.

"Yes. I see you still doing big things." She looked at his chain and watch.

"As I should."

"Who him?" Honey looked thirsty, thinking how many ways she could fuck HD's fat ass to milk him out of some paper because he looked like a true boss.

"We go way back," Rain said, wondering now why he was here, because she heard word that HD had beef with the Scott family. Kanno didn't share their last name, but he was down with them.

"Too far. But I'ma make this quick." HD pulled out a gun from his lower back and shot Honey first in the chest.

"Don't do this, HD, please!" Rain cried.

Boc! Boc! Boc!

The bullets ate into Rain's face before her body fell. HD told Wild to clean it up before leaving. Not too many people knew, but Rain was the first person to ever have sex with HD when he jumped off the porch fresh from D.C.

***

Little Italy, B-more

Kanno had recently brought a nice low key two-bedroom apartment Rags found for him. Only three people knew where he lived: Rags, Egypt, and his girlfriend Pearla.

Since the news of his mother's death, Kanno hadn't said a word. He only shed a few tears. Pearla had been at his crib all day trying to comfort him, but she could tell he was numb and at a loss of thought. When Egypt called with the bad news, Pearla was right there cooking some lunch before having to go back to work for a double shift.

"You okay, baby?" Pearla rubbed his shoulders, hoping to get a word outta him, but got nothing. Looking into his eyes, she saw they looked empty and dark. Pearla got off the bed and figured it would be best to leave him alone until he came around.

"Close the door," he mumbled for the first time and stared into the ceiling in deep thought.

Kanno always had love for his mom because even though she was on drugs heavy, Rain still made sure they had food, clothes, and a roof over their head. There was no doubt in his mind one of his ops killed her, but that would be hard to pinpoint who could have done it. Within time, it would all come to light. He rolled up a blunt of weed and went to sleep.

***

Police station, B-more

Dozen walked in with his morning coffee and bop in his walk. Last night he fucked a bad Spanish bitch and a sexy dark-skinned chick, both from Houston, Texas.

"Dozen!" a fat cop hollered.

"Hey Dozen," a thick new white female cop stated, walking by with tight work pants on. She had a phat ass like a black woman, but was a nun with the pussy.

Walking past some booths, he saw Fatima sitting down doing some file work.

"Hey niece." Dozen pulled up on her to see the evil look on her face.

"Please don't call me that. Better yet, don't call me period," Fatima shot back

"Sorry about Sunny. I heard you was first on the scene."

"Yeah."

"The streets is all some people know, so don't kick yourself down."

"Thanks for your kind words. Now please leave me alone?" she asked.

"Will do, but I'm not your enemy," he told her.

"Maybe not, but you are the one who touched on me when I was a little girl." She saw his face frown.

"Listen here, you little spoiled bitch, you tell anybody about that, you gonna regret it." He pointed a finger in Fatima's face.

"Dozen, I don't fear your threats, and trust me, one day you will pay for what you done," she threatened.

"I'll be waiting," Dozen stated as his captain called him over.

"Dozen, come in, have a seat. I see you speaking to the rookie. She got good work ethics," Captain White stated.

"I'm sure she does. But how's the fam?" Dozen changed the subject.

"Everybody is good. I can't complain. I live a regular white man life with a few affairs and drinks on the daily." He laughed at his own joke.

"That's the best life, boss." Dozen hated kissing ass, but he could tell his captain was fishing.

"I didn't see you at Officer Haper's funeral this past weekend"

"Huh?" He caught Dozen off guard.

"Your co-worker's funeral." Captain White lifted his eyebrows, a little shocked that Dozen out of all people wasn't there because they were so close.

"My nephew had caught the COVID-19 shit and almost died in the hospital." Dozen came up with the first lie he could think of.

"Oh shit, sorry to hear that. COVID-19 killed my mom, uncle, and brother within the same month," Captain White said, looking at a picture of his mom on his desk.

"I send my regards to your family, boss."

"Thanks. But there is something I want you to look into."

"What's that? Anything"

"Look into this Haper case, because I think someone close to him had to have killed him and his family because it don't make sense to me," Captain White said.

"Why do you think that, boss?"

"Because as long as I've known Haper, he never even told me where he lived at, and it seems to me as if someone invited the guests inside."

"You think so?" Dozen moved around in his chair uncomfortably.

"I've been a cop thirty years, Dozen, and when somebody comes to kill or rob, they will kick in the door or use some type of force." Captain White saw Dozen moving around like he had ants in his pants.

"Maybe you right. It could have been a family member."

"Or a close friend." Captain White gave Dozen a strong look.

"I'ma do some research for you, Cap."

"Thanks. We gotta get his killer off the streets because the feds want the case."

"Feds?" Dozen was shocked.

"Yeah."

"I'm on it, boss."

"Okay. Get this sick fuck off the street, Dozen. You and Longhead got this," Captain White said.

Dozen thought about Longhead, who he hadn't seen in days.

Chapter 38
USP Canaan, PA
Months later

Bigs went out to the prison yard on the rec move, missing chow to meet up with Walter, a nigga from his hood in B-more. Bigs had been on the countdown with less than a year left on his sentence. He had been chilling out, trying to make it home.

"Damn, shawty, you gained some weight." Bigs smiled, embracing Walter who had gained weight and grown out a beard.

"Shit, nigga, it's been forever," Walter stated.

"What unit you in?"

"F2. I'm over there with Ty, Rob, VDog, O, and Pull," Walter said, walking the track, looking at the towers in the middle of the yard as the guards waited for something to pop off.

"Okay, you're in good hands. How long they gave you for that shit?"

Walter had a shootout with police after being caught red-handed killing a nigga next to a police station. When the surrounded him a block away as he tried to run on foot, Walter shot it out with the police, killing one of them. The boys shot Walter seven times, but somehow, he made it to go straight to prison once leaving the hospital.

"They gave me sixty-seven years, bro," Walter stated sadly.

"Damn, bro. Don't worry. You gonna give that time back," Bigs remained positive about his situation.

"Inshallah. But I heard rags and Kanno out there fucking up the town after Five's and Sunny's deaths," said Walter.

"Maybe. I ain't reach out in a few months, but they send money and pics monthly to me."

"That's love, yo. But them little niggas out there warring with X and HD. I heard it's bad, bro."

"I'm sure Rags got it under control. He always been the mastermind type," Bigs said thinking back to when they were kids and Rags always had a plan and plot to something.

The friends talked about the good days until it was rec recall and they went back to their unit.

***

South, B-more

Sha posted on Bank Street with a few of his boys, getting to the money on a late night. The corner store was open until 2 a.m., so niggas trapped there all day like it was the 80's.

Polo and Sha weren't seeing eye to eye but regardless, that was still his boy and connect. This morning, Polo dropped off some work to Sha and told him he planned to start being in the field more once he took care of something.

"I'm 'bout to go inside. Get with me a little later so we can bust down the work," Sha told Solid and Gee before walking into his building.

Sha lived on the third floor and he was high and drunk off Henny walking upstairs, so he paid no attention to the nigga in a black hoodie walking downstairs. With a swift motion, the hooded man pulled out a knife and shoved it into Sha's gut repeatedly until Sha's body got stiff . By the time Kanno was done stabbing, Sha he got hit forty-one times.

Kanno smoothly left Sha's dead body slumped on the staircase while walking off calmly. Outside, he made a left, avoiding the small crowd to his right in front of the corner store selling drugs. Kanno stopped and came up with a quick idea that made him grin.

Boc!

Boc!

Boc!

Boc!

Boc!

Spraying into the crowd, he hit Gee and somebody else as everybody took off running around the corner to save themselves. Kanno ran up the block and jumped in the passenger seat of a black Jeep Fat P was driving.

"I thought no gunplay," Fat P said, busting a U-turn and racing up the block in a Trackhawk speed demon.

"Had to send a message. We been laying low for a while, bro," said Kanno, wiping off his Glock 19 handgun.

"Polo gonna be sick his muscle gone. I can't wait to hear his reaction. Shit, we can take his block now."

"He may let niggas take his ass now, dude so pussy," Kanno said, laughing hard.

***

Washington D.C.

X took Jena out to eat in the beautiful area of downtown D.C. where they had Go-Go clubs, comedy clubs, shopping areas, and classy bars.

"What made you wanna come out here tonight?" asked Jena, wearing a crop top Chanel dress with red lipstick, looking overly alluring.

X wore a clean suit with a sharp shape up on his beard and hairline. "Just wanted to get outta town for a second," X lied. The truth of the matter was that the B-more crime rate been going higher day by day and niggas wanted him dead, so he had to move smart. D.C. was the only place he could travel to without security.

Business had been going downhill because Kanno and this Rags kid he'd been hearing about were flooding the city with good Piru heroin unlike everybody else's dope, which was cut.

"Is that right?" She frowned, finishing her meal

"You been having a crazy attitude lately, Jena. Is everything ok?"

"How long do you plan to do this?"

"Do what? Live happily and wealthy?" He smiled, knowing what she was getting at.

"No, risking your life."

"Jena, I'ma be out the game soon. I just need a little time to tie my loose ends, love," X said.

"You promise, X? Because this ain't the life I want."

"I know, Jena. I promise, a few more months and I'm out."

"Okay, I'ma take your word for it."

"As you should, beautiful. Now how's work?" X asked, happy she got off that subject.

"Work is going well. I met a young man who has been buying a lot of property around the city and reselling it for a broker fee, if not higher."

"He seems smart. What's his name?"

"Doug. He's a great guy, babe." Jena smiled when thinking about him.

"Let's get ready to go home. I need some good loving," X said, looking at her banging gym body.

"I'm ready to give you some good whap."

"Now you're talking,"

"Oh , I am." She laughed getting up to leave.

X paid the bill and escorted his wife outside, thinking about this Doug dude who made his wife blush just at the sound of his name. He knew his wife too well, and if he didn't pay her more attention, then Jena could easily slide off.

***

Fells Point, B-more

Rags and Carena enjoyed the meal Carena made for dinner. This was Rags' second time over here and he loved the way her apartment was set up.

"That shit was good, baby."

Rags and Carena made shit official last night. At first, Carena was a little shaken up about him being a criminal due to her job title, but she had never stopped loving Rags, even when he got arrested. Rags told Carena he was in the street life, but that was all he could go into detail about, and she respected it.

"Thank you, daddy." She picked up his plate and brought it into the kitchen.

"You work this weekend?"

"No, why?"

"I want to take you somewhere," he said, seeing her phat ass through her clear gown.

"You trying to fly me out?"

"Facts. We need a few days away from all the drama."

"Yesss. I'm still on my period, but I think it will be over in a few days."

"A'ight, because I'ma need some of that kitty."

"It's all yours." She sat in his lap. "I'm still working on that Sean P case, but somehow, the Baby Blood file disappeared the other day." She gave him a smile, letting Rags know she had him covered.

"That's my girl."

"Always. But don't worry too much about that Sean cat, Something tells me he will have a long winter"

"Well, I hope someone gives that fucker a slow death."

She kissed him and went to take a shower before going to bed.

***

West B-more

HD was leaving the bank after depositing some money for his business account, something he did every Friday morning. HD made a left at the green light, using his blinker, on his way to check Sean P.

Red and blue lights flashed behind him. He pulled over, hoping it wasn't for him, but when he parked near the curb, so did the cop car.

"Shit, man." HD hid his gun on the side of his seat and got all his papers and license ready.

A female cop approached, wearing a coat and a hat covering half of her face so he could barely see her. The officer knocked at the tinted windows and HD rolled it down and handed her his info without looking into her face.

"Sir, this is you?" The female cop now got a good look at HD's face as they locked eyes.

When HD saw her, it clicked who she was: the woman that Sunny tried to save before he killed him.

Fatima reached for her work gun, but HD was more seasoned.

Boc! Boc! Boc! Boc!

Boom! Boom!

They both shot each other. Fatima got hit twice in the vest, but caught him once in the chest before he pulled off. Fatima caught her breath and called it in on her walkie-talkie undoing the vest that stopped the bullets.

Chapter 39
PG county, B-more

Sean P cleaned his house, awaiting a chick who was on her way over. He had been trying to fuck this bitch for months, but she was playing hard to get until he bought her a Birkin bag and a Benz coupe. Sean P finally won her over today. She texted him and said she wanted some dick, and it better be good.

The last couple of months, Sean P had been getting more money in D.C. than B-more due to the ongoing war. He still had a few blocks, but his enemy had better product, and the man with the best work always won. That was the game.

His main worry was the feds picking him up. Ever since he tried to kidnap that DA chick Carena and failed at his attempt, he had been laying low. Seeing Rags pop up was the last thing on his mind that day and almost caused him to lose his life.

Hearing the doorbell, Sean P checked himself out in his living room mirror, feeling cocky as usual. Looking at the ice bucket on the table with two bottles of Moet, he knew it would be a night to remember.

Opening the door, he saw Erica standing there wide-legged in a red and white designer dress, leaving him speechless. Her hips were so wide it looked like pillows and Erica had a flat stomach to match. She was a high yellow female, thick, curvy, long blonde hair that she dyed, soft hazel eyes, a cute nose piercing, and the sexiest smile. Sean P looked at her pretty white manicured toes then up to Erica's nice perky breasts, which he pictured himself sucking on.

"You gonna stare or let me in, blood hound," she joked.

"I can't help but to stare at my next plate of food," he flirted.

"The first taste may have you going crazy," she shot back, walking inside the polished mansion, impressed.

"It's worth it, I bet." He watched the way her ass moved as if she had no panties on underneath the way it was clapping and giggling with each step.

"This spot is nice."

"This ain't nothing. I'm about to buy a spot three times bigger in North Carolina," said Sean P, sitting down.

"I always wanted to move down there."

"Maybe if you play your cards right, you can come with me."

"Oh yeah? That sounds cool."

"Let me go get some glasses." Sean P felt his manhood eager to escape his pants, but he controlled it, walking towards the large kitchen.

"Okay." She relaxed.

"You like your new Benz?"

"Yes, thanks. How could I ever repay you?" Erica's voice got sexy.

"I could think of a few things," said Sean P, coming out of the kitchen smirking with glasses. Sean P made it back into the living room area and dropped the glasses on the floor. "What the fuck?" He didn't know what to do at the sight of Erica pointing a gun at him. "Erica, you tripping, right?"

"Bum-ass nigga, my name's not Erica. Call me Egypt or your death maker. You killed my mother, and I'm here to collect," Egypt stated.

The first week she met Sean P, he bragged about all his murders when she told him how much she love gangstas. One murder he mentioned about a woman named Rain caught her ear and ever since then, Egypt had been waiting to seek revenge in her mom's death. The irony was that Sean P had been lying about killing Rain. He was just capping in order to boost good gangsta on her eyes. Now, he regretted it.

"Look, bitch you got the wrong nigga," he spat.

"Rain. Sound familiar?" She got closer, but still kept a distance.

"That crackhead bitch? Yo, I ain't kill her. My people did."

"Well, I guess you will pay for their mistake with your blood."

"Bitch, you ain't gonna do—"

Bloc!

Bloc!

Bloc!

Bloc!

Bloc!

"Stupid-ass nigga," Egypt said, taking his rings, chains, and watch off him. She planned to give it to Kanno for his birthday tomorrow.

***

Downtown, B-more

The next night, Kanno celebrated his birthday at a lounge located downtown. He bought out the bar and all the VIP booths. His crew was fifty deep, all having a good time. The only one he was missing was Bigs, who still had a few months left on his sentence.

It was winter time, so everybody rocked nice sweaters, Dior sweat suits, and fly suits. Kanno had recently proposed to Pearla, so she was on cloud nine preparing a wedding.

"I can't believe it's your birthday, bro," Rags said.

"Yo, I can't believe we made it this far," Fat P added, looking for a bottle girl to bring more liquor.

"This is only a start, shawty. By the summer, the city will be ours."

All three men saw a beautiful thick woman coming their way through the dim lights.

"What the fuck is she doing here?" Kanno said, knowing that walk from anywhere.

Rags was in love with Carena, but the woman coming his way put him in a different state of mind until she got closer. He was mad at himself.

"Happy Birthday, brother." Egypt gave him a hug.

"Thanks, sis."

"Egypt? I had no clue that was you," Rags said.

"Hey Rags." She blushed because since she was a little girl, she always had a crush on Rags.

"What, you got your body done or something?" Fat P let the liquor do the talking, looking at his little cousin, trying to figure out how she got so thick and bad.

"Nigga, shut up," Kanno said.

"I go to the gym, fat ass. Maybe you should try it." She made everybody laugh

"Fuck the gym. I can go get some lipo." He was serious

"Anyway, I came to give you this gift, but open it when I leave. This club life ain't for me so I'm gone, but I love y'all. See you around, Rags," Egypt looked Rags in his eyes, reading his thoughts before walking out.

Rags had to admit Egypt had grown up into a beautiful woman. If he wasn't locked in with Carena, then she would be number one on his hit list.

Kanno opened the jewelry box to see rings, chains, and a watch with bloodstains on it.

"What the hell?" Kanno lifted the chain up, wondering where he had seen it before.

"Yo, that's Sean P's shit." Fat P remembered seeing it on his op's neck several times.

"You right, shawty." Kanno looked confused and lost as to why Egypt would bring him this. Kanno's cell phone received a text message and he opened it to see Sean P on the floor in a puddle of blood. "Check this shit out." Kanno handed Rags his phone.

"Ain't no way, bro." Rags couldn't believe it. Either Egypt was a killer, or she had gotten their rival knocked off.

"We need cuz on the team," Fat P said.

"She most likely had someone else do this. We all know my little sister ain't capable of this type of shit." Kanno stared at the picture

"At least we hope not," Rags corrected him.

***

Queens, NY

Rags came out to a baseball game at the MetLife stadium to meet up with North. This would be his third time coming out to New York alone to meet the plug since Sunny died. North and Abdullah wanted to send goons to Baltimore so they could kill whoever murdered Sunny and Five. Rags explained to them patience was a must and he would kill all of them, but it was about timing. Abdullah understood, but North didn't. He wanted to see blood spill for his family.

The drugs Rags was getting had the city of Baltimore in a state of emergency. A lot of fiends weren't cutting the heroin correctly and would overdose, not realizing how strong the dope was until it became too late.

North had on a Mets outfit. He walked through the aisle. Not a lot of people came out today so they were out of earshot from civilians.

"What's up, cuz?" North said, giving Rags some dap.

"You a Mets fan, I see."

"Never. I loved the Yankees since I was a kid,"

"Shit, I can't really tell,"

"Gotta switch it up. But everything is in place. A black Honda with a JFC 142 license plate will be following you. What car did you drive up in?"

"A blue Hellcat Redeye."

"Great getaway car."

"Question: where the fuck are y'all getting this dog food from, shawty? Because that shit got people going crazy, dying, and loving this shit, my nigga, I kid you not."

"Rags, we family and all that, but if I told you, son, then I'd have to kill you," North stated.

"Oh, okay."

"Nah, I'm joking, cuz. We get out shit straight from the land."

"The land? What the fuck is that?" Rags seemed lost.

"Africa, nigga."

"Oh shit, no wonder why that shit so pure, bro." Rags had heard stories about how Africa had the best heroin in the world besides the Middle East.

"Our family out there is doing big things, you heard? I'm surprised Proof ain't put you on, boy."

"Nah, but when I go see him, I'ma ask." Rags planned to visit his dad next weekend on the west coast.

"Say that, bro. But I gotta go. My dad sick."

"He gonna be good?"

"I hope so," North said, leaving.

Chapter 40
East side, B-more

A block away from Monument East, Dozen sat in the undercover car watching his next target. He was counting on Longhead to show up, but something had popped up on his behalf where he couldn't come out. Lately, Dozen peeped how funny his partner had been acting, but he tried to look past it.

The last two weeks had been amazing for Dozen. He robbed two spots and came out with the motherlode. The traps belonged to a new hustler Dozen barely knew named Polo. Even the building he was staking out now belonged to Polo and his crew.

Dozen took the last puff of exotic weed and blew out, wondering why he didn't see people running in and out as he did any other time. Pulling the hoodie over his head, he got in the car and walked toward the building, acting like a civilian. The front door was cracked, leading into a hallway that had two apartment doors. Both apartments were used to sell drugs out of, he knew for a fact, so he picked the one to his left.

"Fuck it, worth the try." Dozen pulled out his pistol and cocked it back, reaching for the doorknob.

It was unlocked already. Dozen rushed into the empty crib with his weapon out to see nothing except an old rug and dirty curtains. A cold metal object was pressed to the back of his head catching him completely off guard.

"Greed is what took out the best kings in the ancient times. Lower your gun real slow," a voice stated behind him.

"This is police work; I'm a cop. You're making a big mistake."

"You already made the mistake by robbing my spots, Dozen. Now put your weapon down before I blow your head the fuck off," Polo said.

Dozen knew he was caught, so he followed orders. "You got it. But how did you know?" Dozen wanted to know because there were only a few people who knew about his recent robbing spree.

"I guess I can tell you now that I'ma kill you anyway. Longhead approached me with a recorded video of you bragging on robbing my spots," Polo admitted.

"That pussy!" Dozen was furious.

"Don't worry about him He's in the same boat as you because I wouldn't be able to trust him after this. You see, Dozen, I'm a smart killer, which means I only kill when it's called for and calculated."

"Makes sense. I guess." Dozen still had his back turned.

"See you soon."

Bloc! Bloc! Bloc! Bloc! Bloc!

Dozen's body fell face first into the carpet as smoke steamed from the back of his head. Polo's goons came out of the other apartment to clean up the mess. If Dozen would have gone into the other apartment where Polo's goons were, then he told them to tie him up until he walked over to finish the job.

Polo paid Longhead a lot of money to receive info on Dozen robbing his spots. When giving Longhead the money, Polo had another plan for Longhead, which was death.

***

Victorville USP, Cali

Rags came out to pay a visit to his dad in jail. On his way out to the west coast. He got a call saying Dozen's body was found in a build on the east side of town.

He was starting to feel like everybody around him was either dying or getting ghost. Now it was just him and his crew on deck. Bigs was on his way home soon, so that would put the crew together.

Proof walked out with his old school bop, smiling to see his baby boy there. At first, he thought his appeal lawyer came down to decide their motion he was about to put in.

"You look like me, young'un," Proof said, giving his son a hug.

"Yeah. I been gaining weight."

"A lot been going on, I'm hearing." Proof got serious.

"Dozen just died."

"Damn. How the fuck y'all keep letting them niggas kill ours?" Proof got mad.

"We working on it, Pops. I'm trying. Niggas be hiding. I'm on it, trust me."

"Trusting anybody nowadays is the worst thing I could do, so I prefer to give you the benefit of the doubt, son, because if I feel like you crossed me, the trust and honor I had will vanish."

"I respect that. But all I got is my word."

"True dat. Kanno's brother is my celly, Nice."

"Oh shit, it's been awhile. But I'm going to tell Kanno. I remember he used to be cool with Sunny"

"Yeah." Proof's voice saddened.

"Fatima doing good."

"I speak to her a few times a week. I'm proud of my baby. She is making something outta herself," Proof said.

"I've met Abdullah."

"My brother got his ways, but he heavy on family and loyalty," Proof said, looking at a female CO smiling at him. She was the one giving him drugs to sell in the prison.

"How come you never told me about the African side of the family?"

"Some things in life have a time period, and that was one of them," Proof explained.

"I understand."

"My brother got cancer, so I don't know how long he got to live, but it's bad." Proof recently found out the news about Abdullah a few days ago.

"I ain't really know. North stated something about his well-being, but I had no clue it was that serious." Rags sounded concerned.

"Stick with family. They got the best product out there."

"I know now. They always on perfect timing"

"Good, but invest your time in getting rid of your enemy. The money ain't going nowhere, but if your op catches up with you, then there won't be no enjoying money and your success."

"Sure you're right, Pops. In due time."

The visit lasted another hour.

***

Downton, B-more

Fat P and a few of his goons came out to a hookah bar, enjoying the night.

"This spot is turned up tonight, bro," Chatty said. He was a close friend of Fat P's since youth.

"I told you this shit was jumping, shawty." Fat P gulped down a bottle of Henny.

"Facts."

"You heard about that cop killing?" Chatty asked.

"Shit, the whole city knows about Dozen, big bro. He was shady, but for the team," Fat P stated.

"For the team?"

"Yeah. He worked for Sunny and Five when they were getting money." Fat P's voice slurred a little.

"Damn, I had no clue, shawty," Chatty said, seeing niggas entering the dark side of the club.

"Who dem niggas?" asked Fat P. He tried to look to see who the gang was entering the club.

"I see some nigga with glasses," one of Fat P's young boys said.

When Fat P saw X and a group of niggas walk in, he jumped up, racing towards the opps. The security guards at the gates had taken all of the crew's guns because they didn't want violence.

The crew blocked off X's crew. Both sides had an equal amount of men. Fat P and X were face to face now.

"I know you, little nigga?" X asked, looking at Fat P, already knowing who he was a part of Rags' crew.

"You about to." Fat P punched X in the face, almost making him stumble backwards.

X's goons started fighting with Fat P's crew as the club went up, going crazy. Everybody started fighting. X pulled out a gun and shot Fat P twice in the pelvic area, making him drop to the floor.

The partygoers took off running, causing chaos, making people scream out of fear, heading for the exit.

The police and ambulances came on time and they carried Fat P out of the club.

***

North, B-more

Fatima got a call from the police station saying a car parked in the parking lot had a strong odor to it and needed to be moved.

Driving to the area, the thought of Dozen came across her mind and she laughed to herself. She understood karma came in all shapes and forms.

Pulling into the area, she saw a gray Chevy parked in the middle of a lot. Fatima hopped out and looked at the car, smelling a strong smell she couldn't grasp.

"What the fuck is that smell?" she said to herself.

Fatima opened the car's driver side door and the scent hit her a lot worse than the outside. Looking through the back, she saw nothing, but she could tell the odor was coming from the back area. She popped the trunk and walked to the back.

Fatima almost caught a heart attack when she saw Longhead's body with mice and insects crawling all over. She recognized the detective's face even though the six bullet holes and blood had taken most of his facial features.

She called it in and backed away from the car, trying to catch up on her breathing.

Chapter 41
North, B-more

Kanno pulled up to Pearla's crib with a new car because too many people knew about his other whip, so he had to switch up. He hadn't seen Pearla in a few days, so he wanted to pay her a visit and spend time with shawty.

Last night, he went to visit Fat P in the hospital and his boy was in bad condition to the point that the doctor said Fat P might never walk away. Fat P told him X did it at the club when a fight broke out between the two crews. Kanno told his boy in due time he would handle X, but right now, they had a bunch of other shit going on.

Walking in Pearla's building he saw she had left the door open for him. The smell of fried chicken came from the hallways. He loved her cooking. Pearla cooked her ass off every time he came over here. She made sure her man ate a full meal.

"Hey baby." Kanno entered, seeing she was in the living room area with her pretty feet out, watching a wedding TV show.

"I made you dinner, my love," she said, kissing his lips, then seeing a familiar necklace, watch, and rings.

"Thanks, babe, I'm starving," he stated, seeing Pearla zone in on his jewelry. "You like?" He lifted the chain Egypt gave him on his birthday.

"Yeah, it's nice. Where did you get it?" she asked.

"A gift."

"Let me see." Pearla had to make sure her mind wasn't lying. She turned the chain around and saw the words SP on the lock area. Pearla went with Sean P the day he went to pick up his necklace from a jewelry store in D.C. years ago. That's how she remembered the SP brand on the lock.

"I'ma get you one after our wedding day." Kanno sat down in front of his plate, missing Pearla's cold stares.

***

Southside, B-more

Baby Blood rocked an all-red outfit today with a red bandana hanging from his right side as he jumped out of the red Porsche, something new for the end of winter.

He had a nice thick dark-skinned chick in the passenger seat whom he had met last night in VA and brought back with him. Baby Blood had been moving around in other states, selling kilos to expand Rags' empire. Baby Blood figured since he had so many hitters and soldiers, why not let them run the Baltimore streets while he focused on other areas like VA, Philly, and New Jersey? With a lot of Blood homies in different states, he was making big moves.

"I'ma be right back," Baby Blood told the woman next to him before going into the building. He came over to her passenger window.

"Okay. I'll be here waiting." She blew him a kiss.

Once a week, he would come check up on his traps, then he would link up with Rags or Kanno. The bond between the two men started off rocky, but now Baby Blood started to take a liking to Kanno. With traveling in and outta state, Baby Blood couldn't make time for his own kids and family. Once leaving here, he planned to drop off the female he came with at a hotel and go spend time with his children.

Stepping inside the trap house located on a dead-end block Baby Blood saw nobody, which didn't make sense to him because there were supposed to be at least four or five dudes present all day watching over the drugs and money.

"Shawty, Roc, and PG!" he shouted for his goons, walking around the building, seeing and hearing nothing.

Something told him to check the bathroom area and when he did, Baby Blood almost vomited on himself. There were three niggas shoved into the tub full of blood and one of the victims was his little brother, who came around from time to time to chill with PG, who was the same age as him. Baby Blood had tears in his eyes as he walked out the front door then the craziest shit happened

"Freeze! FBI! FBI!" A dozen red dots pointed to his chest.

Baby Blood put his hands up in the air with nowhere to go. He saw the woman he had in the car was front line with an FBI coat and badge.

The woman he met in VA was a federal agent from VA who was sent out to wheel Baby Blood under RICO for the drug trafficking in VA. Since the Baltimore FBI dropped the case on Baby Blood the VA federal build picked it up and built a stronger case.

"The agents cuffed Baby Blood and took him to a black van with a cage in the back.

"You thought you was about to get some pussy, huh?" The woman he brought to B-more said laughed, placing him in the van.

"Your shit look like it stank anyway."

"Well, what would you prefer, a stank pussy or man ass? Better yet, I'ma leave that question alone." She laughed, slamming the door on him.

***

Downtown, B-more

HD spent the weekend at his condo, sniffing coke and fucking stripper bitches he brought out from D.C.

Life had been so fucked that HD hadn't had time to focus on himself, so he made this weekend, which was his birthday, one that he turned up.

The women were asleep all over the place. He was about to wake up two of them for a little threesome party until he heard a knock at the front door. He took a sniff of coke and went to answer it, hoping it was more women arriving because he had grown sick of the ones already there in a matter of hours.

HD opened the door in his robe only to be tackled to the floor by a big muscle-headed white boy wearing a vest and an FBI uniform.

"You're under arrest for murder and kingpin status under the federal law."

The other agents ran into the condo arresting the high and drunk strippers.

HD was so high he thought this whole scene was a movie being filmed, but the more he looked around, the more reality started to hit him. Outside, he saw Baltimore Fox 45 News and a few other stations all surrounding the expensive building, taking pictures as he kept his head down with HD's fat stomach exposed.

Carena was the lead DA on the HD case, which meant a big promotion for her. The FBI had been trying to crack HD for years, but couldn't find enough solid factors to indict him. She found out about the killing of Sunny through the diner video footage. The footage showed HD's face hanging out the window as he tried to shoot at a uniformed cop while killing Sunny.

Finding things leading back to ten years ago, Carena was able to build a solid case on HD, which would most likely get him a life sentence with all twenty-six of the serious counts and charges against him.

***

South east, B-more
Months later

Bigs waited outside his grandma's house after coming home from prison with his weight up, waiting on Rags to pull up with Kanno. He touched down in town five hours ago off his bus. Bigs could have had his boys pick him up, but he waited to come home in peace and to clear his mind on the ride there.

The city looked different after being gone close to five years, but he felt that was a good thing. Bigs had a job lined up with his uncle doing construction for the city. Bigs had done a lot of thinking this past year and he didn't want to get back into the street life. After seeing his boy Dex from New York in Canaan USP fight his life sentence and other brothers like a Muslim brother name Khalid from New York, Bigs just wanted to live a regular life, and he planned to tell his crew, hoping they understood.

A Hellcat Redeye pulled up with a loud engine. He saw Rags and Kanno both with big smiles as they got out of the muscle car with bags of clothes and sneakers. While meeting them halfway, a

SUV pulled up quickly with its windows rolled down, and masked men pointed a Mac-10 and a Draco towards them.

Rags peeped the look on Bigs' face and turned around to see the shit was about to pop off. He hit the ground, pushing Kanno down also. He was slipping, happy to see Bigs.

Tat! Tat! Tat! Tat! Tat! Tat! Tat!

Bullets caught Bigs as he didn't know what to do in the midst of things. Having been away from the streets for so long, Bigs forgot how to duck bullets. Rags rushed to Bigs' aid as the SUV peeled off while Kanno chased it down in the middle of the block.

Boom!

Boom!

Boom!

Boom!

The SUV's back window busted out and the truck swerved into a light pole next to a high school. Kanno ran down the block to finish the job, but when he arrived at the crime scene, all three young men were dead in the truck. Running back over to Rags and Bigs, he heard sirens, making him nervous. From the tears rolling down Rags' face, he could tell Bigs was gone.

"They on their way," said Kanno, trying to hold back his own emotions while looking at Bigs' bloody white tee on the pavement.

Rags snapped outta his zone and ran to the Hellcat as Kanno hopped inside and they bounced before the police arrived at the scene.

Not only was Bigs dead, but his grandmother was in the living room window watching Rags and Kanno before the gun battle took place. Six bullets entered the crib and two of the stray rounds hit Bigs' grandmom in her chest, killing her on the way to the nearby hospital.

The whole southeast loved Ms. Wells. The news of her death sparked an outrage in the city. She was a loyal member of the local church, city hall, and the Board of Education.

Chapter 42
Fells Point, B-more

Fatima woke up with a light hangover from drinking wine with Tavon last night, then one thing led to another. He made good love to Fatima all night. It was something her body had been yearning for.

She barely saw Tavon nowadays, but he explained that due to his new job driving 18 wheeler trucks, he had to always be on the road. Fatima understood because her job consisted of most of her life also, and he understood that as well.

"Morning, babe." Tavon walked back into the room with a nice Rolex watch she had never seen him wear before.

"Hey, where you off to?" Fatima sat up in her huge bed, stretching.

"I'ma go pay my grandmom a visit." His comeback was quick.

"I thought your grandmom passed last year due to COVID-19." Fatima remembered because Tavon was emotionally hurt behind her death for a few weeks.

"Oh no, that was my other grandmom," Tavon shot back, putting on his Timbs.

"Do you want me to come? We will be able to spend some more time together," she suggested.

"It's fine. I'ma call you when I get back, big head." He kissed Fatima on her cheeks, then left without uttering another word.

Fatima felt something in her body saying to follow him because something seemed off. In college when they first met, Tavon told her he only had one grandmom, which was the woman who recently passed.

She didn't want to feel like a stalker, so she tried not to overthink it, but Fatima felt like there was a piece of the puzzle missing.

Fatima jumped up and called her best friend Lindsay from college, who worked as an FBI agent, to run Tavon's name.

Rushing to get dressed, Fatima went to an app that could tell where Tavon was at all times, somewhat like a location GPS tracker.

When she placed the GPS tracker on his phone, Fatima did it for his safety just in case something ever happened to him, but now she was using it for her own cause.

***

Downtown, B-more

It only took Tavon, a.k.a. Polo, a few minutes to arrive at his destination at a low-key deck near the river for his meeting. Not too many people knew Polo by his real name Tavon besides his girl Fatima, whom he had been on and off with since college. Polo dropped outta college to pursue the street life instead of basketball. All his childhood friends like Sha were already in the game hard body, making big names for themselves.

When Fatima became a cop, Polo had to create a distance with her just so she wouldn't get a hint of what he was really on. Polo had love for Fatima but regardless, he was a drug dealer and she lived her life as a cop, so he could never trust Fatima.

Polo parked next to a Bentley coupe, already knowing who the luxury whip belonged to. He walked to the end of the water deck to see X standing there with a briefcase, rocking a suit and tie.

"Polo, young brother, nice to finally meet you." X shook his hand.

"Likewise, old head."

"Old head? Boy, I'll run circles around you," X joked.

"Maybe. But what's the reason for the small get together?" Polo looked at the briefcase.

"I thought you'd never ask. I want you to join me and take over the city. We took out the main players already. There are only a few left." X spoke of Rags and Kanno.

"HD and Baby Blood are locked up and them savages already took over their blocks," Polo said.

"That's the easy part. Money will make anybody turn a blind eye." X handed Polo the briefcase filled with money.

Polo looked inside and saw X reach for his gun, watching someone come from behind.

“Drop your weapon. Baltimore PD!” a familiar voice yelled to X as Polo turned around to see Fatima.

“Fatima, what are you doing here?” Polo asked, shocked and caught.

“This is what you’re into?” Fatima almost had tears in her eyes.

“Look, babe, put the gun down and we can talk about this” Polo said

“Polo, get your bitch!” X yelled, pointing his gun at Fatima.

“Drop the gun!” Fatima yelled to X with her finger on the trigger. A shadow appeared outta nowhere.

Bloc! Bloc! Bloc! Bloc! Bloc! Bloc!

Fatima and Polo saw X’s body get riddled with bullets as he fell into the water. Rags appeared out of the shadows and Polo reached for his gun, dropping the briefcase.

Fatima saw Rags’ P89 Ruger jam as he tried to fire on Polo. Fatima had one or two choices.

Boc! Boc! Boc! Boc!

Polo’s chest got filled with Glock 19 rounds and a clean head shot, making him drop where he stood. Fatima quickly called it into the station before taking Polo’s gun and firing two shots into the air.

“Rags, go now!” she yelled, not wanting him caught up in this double homicide.

“You good?”

“Yes. Leave,” she demanded, hearing police sirens closing in on them.

***

Fells Points, B-more

Rags and Carena both were getting ready to go their separate ways. Rags had a trip to New York and Carena had a meeting with the new federal bosses, a white woman and man named Lindsay and Matthew.

“Babe, they got a new bitch taking over the FBI. Her name is Lindsey and from what I’ve heard, she a beast,” Carena said, trying to give her boo the heads up.

"A'ight. After this trip to New York, I'ma slid outta town for a while," he stated.

"We leaving," she corrected him.

"What time you get off?"

"At 9 p.m., babe."

"I'ma be back by then." Rags kissed her and left her crib.

Carena felt something wasn't right in the back of her head, but she was also on her period and around these times, she always overthought shit.

***

Brooklyn, NY

Hours later, Rags arrived at the Barclay Center to meet North for the next drug transaction. The establishment was a sight to see. As he was walking to a restaurant, North texted him.

North had a table in the front section with another woman Rags had seen too many times. As Rags was coming in, the beautiful brown-skinned woman was getting up to leave. When she walked by Rags, the woman paused.

"Hey Doug, what a surprise to see you here," Jena said.

"I should be saying the same." Rags couldn't believe he was face to face with the woman he'd been doing real estate business with since he'd been out from prison.

"Take care. I'll see you soon." Jena walked off in a nice classy business suit.

Rags couldn't believe who he just ran into, but he sat at the table next to North.

"What's going on, cuzzy?" North stated, wearing a nice outfit.

"I know shawty."

"Yeah, Jena good people. I went to school with her. She was in the city and came to say hi," North told him.

"Okay, that's what's up"

"Business been good, I see."

"Yeah, of course. That's why I'm here now, to load up." Rags smiled.

"We have a small issue today. One of the drivers got pregnant and another one quit, so you gotta take the load yourself," North explained.

"Damn, I wish you would have told me"

"I'm not heavy on talking over the phone. But we can do this another time if you don't wanna travel with it."

"No, I'ma do it, bro."

"You sure?"

"Yes," Rags replied as North sent a text to his goons.

"You're in the black Range Rover?" asked North.

"That's me."

"I'ma have them place it in your trunk."

"Okay, perfect." Rags had no choice but to accept the shitty hand because niggas needed dope.

Lil Heat took over Baby Blood's blocks and was his older cousin so he took control, plus Lil Heat's name in the streets was feared by most. Kanno also needed product so he could take over Polo's block and X's now since they were all outta the picture. Rags and his crew were the last men standing in the city, which made them targets, but they had all the work.

"I spoke with Proof last week," North added.

"Yeah, I went to visit him a few months back."

"So I've heard he's working hard on trying to get out. Unc didn't deserve a life sentence." North shook his head.

"I agree. This game is a hard bargain, bro. But I'ma hit the road so I can make it back on time."

"Okay, son, be safe. I'm here," North said, watching Rags get up to leave.

***

Driving back down I-85 South, Rags turned on some music, HOT 97, a rap radio station. To his surprise, his cell phone died, so he placed it on the car charger.

Police cars and black vans blocked him in on the George Washington Bridge in the middle of the day. Rags saw them drive past, but paid them no mind forgetting what was in the back.

"Fuck, yo." Rags looked for a way out, but he was trapped it had to be twenty cars, vans, and trucks surrounding him with flashing lights.

All types of police agents from NYPD, FBI, ATF, and DEA were out when he stepped out of the truck with his hands high. The police rushed him and put cuffs on Rags, tossing him into the back of an all-black SUV.

He watched the agents go directly to the trunk of his SUV and get the three large duffle bags filled with heroin.

Rags eyes said it all from behind the dark tints. Someone set him up.

***

Downtown, B-more
Meanwhile

"Ladies and gentlemen, today we will embark on a new achievement called the Young Kingpins," Agent Lindsey said in front of more than thirty federal law enforcement and DA's.

When Carena got her folder, she almost shit herself. The first person she saw was Rags' photo as the leader.

"These young men, including the one in the wheelchair, are responsible for most of the city's drug trafficking. They are being charged with a dozen unrelated murders including three Baltimore police officers: Dozen, Longhead, and Haper. Right now the leader is being arrested in New York, thanks to some big help. The rest should be going down any minute, so get your caseloads clear, because you all have a lot to do on this two hundred man indictment - the biggest Baltimore has ever seen. We've teamed up with VA, D.C., and New York. That's how we rolling." Lindsey ended by hearing everybody clap except Carena, who rushed out to call Rags, but she only got a voicemail.

***

Southeast B-more

Fat P was now living outta a wheelchair thanks to his ops, but he planned to make the best outta it. The block was dry today because nobody had any drugs. They were waiting on Rags to come back.

"Push me to the store," he told his personal caretaker, Bo.

On their way to the store, Bo thought he saw an unfamiliar car pull up behind them, but Bo just wanted to hurry back home, where he had some pussy waiting for him.

Fat P bought a bag full of snacks and juices before rolling back down the block, but before he could make it, a gang of law enforcement agents jumped out with assault rifles.

"Fuck dat." Fat P pulled out a Tech 9 from under his lap and opened fire. He told himself he would die in the streets before dying in jail.

Tat, tat, tat, tat, tat, tat, tat, tat, tat!

Two cops caught bullets to the face and neck, but the rest of the cops fired, killing Fat P and Bo. The law enforcement agents shot Fat P so many times that his body fell out of his wheelchair.

***

Manhattan, NY

Rags was cuffed up in a bullpen with a young cat rocking all blue sitting in the corner, upset.

"Mr. Scott," a female cop said, coming to the bars with an arm full of papers.

"Jena?" Rags stated, shocked to see her, wondering if she was a lawyer.

"Rags, we finally got you, dog, but check this out. My name is Agent Flowers. My field name is Jena."

"You set me up," Rags stated.

"No, actually, you set yourself up because I was building a case on X, my late husband, which was ongoing for a few years before you came into the picture. We never wanted you, Doug. When I sold you houses, I thought you were legit. I looked you up to only see a little record, but when I saw you were related to Proof, Five, and Sunny, I watched you. This whole time, it's been your own family setting you up," she said.

"My family? What the fuck you talking about?" Rags yelled and then seconds later, he saw Abdulla and North come in rocking FBI badges.

"You should have come home and focused on real estate, nephew," Abdulla stated, smiling

"Five warned you," North added

"Y'all were pigs the whole time? Does my dad know?"

"Proof didn't know his own brother and nephew were agents, but they are the main reason he is in prison. The only reason why he still don't know is because we couldn't risk our family's lives by exposing our names, but we had to with this case," Abdullah said.

"But we could use your help dealing with some Cartels in Miami. We will take you off the case and put Kanno, HD, and Baby Blood as the kingpins and ship you out to Miami for some big fish. We got faith in you," Jena said, seeing Rags laugh.

"Where is my lawyer?" Rags said

"Okay, see you in court." All three of them walked off in laughter.

"Our lawyer is on the way," the young man wearing all blue said, sitting in the far corner, listening to every word.

"Our lawyer? Who the fuck are you?" Rags asked, getting a closer look at the kid. His eyes looked familiar.

"I'm Zayon. You're my brother. Proof is my da. He just kept me a secret along with my older brother, who is a federal lawyer. He's on his way."

"Ain't no fucking way."

"ReRe, your mom, has known about us for years, Doug. My father said he planned to tell you and Fatima soon until this took place," Zayon said as Rags tried to digest everything.

"Why are you here?" Rags couldn't lie; the kid looked more like Proof than he did.

"I was copping weight from Abdulla, trying to flood New York City.

"Fuck. Our lives are over." Rags sat down on the bench.

"Don't be so fast to call it quits. I got a plan," said Zayon, smiling.

"What could that possibly be?" Rags thought Zayon had lost his mind until hearing it and who would be a part of it.

***

Victorville USP, Cali
One year later

HD walked into unit 5B with a bedroll and a cup full of hygiene items, looking for Baltimore homies. Two months ago he blew trial with forty other co-defendants, but the crazy part was that half of the people on his case were freed due to lost files, lack of evidence, and speedy trials that they won.

When he heard Rags had won his case, he was so mad he couldn't sleep for days after receiving a life sentence plus twenty-two years. Baby Blood also received the same amount of time, mainly because of his VA cases, while the Baltimore federal indictments he beat.

A correctional officer told HD which cell to go into. A nigga from Miami told him all his B-more and D.C. homies were on the yard. HD went inside the cell to see a young man sitting down reading a hood novel called *Murda Season* by author Romell Tukes. He had read a few of his books.

"What up, slim? I'm HD. They sent me up in here. You from the town?"

"Yeah. I'm Nice from southeast." Nice saw the scared look on HD's face, but he kept it to himself.

"That's what's up, slim. I heard a lot about this spot," HD stated.

"This shit ain't bad, yo. But get yourself together. I'ma go get you a mattress." Nice left the cell.

Minutes later, the door opened, and HD thought it was Nice, but when he saw who it was, his heart froze.

"I thought I would never see this day," Proof stated, pulling out a long blade, rushing HD, who stood there with cold feet. Proof started to work HD, stabbing him in his upper torso and heart, killing the big man in a matter of seconds.

Proof tucked his knife and walked out of the cell, where Nice stood.

"Tell the homies to take his body to the showers. The cameras been down all day so we good, shawty," Proof said, walking off to use the jail phone as if nothing had happened.

***

Atlanta, GA
Month later

Rags and Carena moved to Atlanta and loved every bit of it. The city was full of blacks and success. When he beat his federal case, Rags wanted to move away from Baltimore, so it was Carena's idea to move to ATL, plus she had his baby boy on the way.

Zayon came up with a master plan for Abdullah and North with a few murders he knew they did in Brooklyn. The two agents had no choice but to lose some of the files, but that wasn't enough. Rags found out Fatima knew Lindsey so he asked if she could speak with the woman, and his sister came through.

The icing on the case was that Zayon's mom worked as the federal judge who had the federal case, so she looked out for half of the indictment. Some people had so much solid evidence on them she couldn't do anything for them at all. For some people with clean records, she was able to get them five to ten years and some she let free off of a lack of evidence.

"Have you thought of a name yet?" he asked Carena, walking through the mall.

"No, how about you?" Carena looked sexy with a baby about to bust outta her any minute.

"Maybe tonight we can," Rags added as he went into a baby store. This was the life he always wanted to have eventually, but beating the feds and giving them a fight wasn't in his plans, nor was ending up like Baby Blood or worse, Fat P.

Fatima was doing well. Kanno had started a business buying vans to use as carpools for nursing homes. ReRe was back in Baltimore on an appeal, and his dad Proof was coming up soon. One thing Rags didn't mention: he, Zayon, and Egypt, who was Kanno's sister, were flooding the south with good pure dope from their new plug.

The End

Lock Down Publications and Ca$h Presents assisted publishing packages.

BASIC PACKAGE $499
Editing
Cover Design
Formatting

UPGRADED PACKAGE $800
Typing
Editing
Cover Design
Formatting

ADVANCE PACKAGE $1,200
Typing
Editing
Cover Design
Formatting
Copyright registration
Proofreading
Upload book to Amazon

LDP SUPREME PACKAGE $1,500
Typing
Editing
Cover Design
Formatting
Copyright registration
Proofreading
Set up Amazon account
Upload book to Amazon
Advertise on LDP Amazon and Facebook page

***Other services available upon request. Additional charges may apply

Lock Down Publications
P.O. Box 944
Stockbridge, GA 30281-9998
Phone # 470 303-9761

Submission Guideline

Submit the first three chapters of your completed manuscript to ldpsubmissions@gmail.com, subject line: Your book's title. The manuscript must be in a .doc file and sent as an attachment. Document should be in Times New Roman, double spaced and in size 12 font. Also, provide your synopsis and full contact information. If sending multiple submissions, they must each be in a separate email.

Have a story but no way to send it electronically? You can still submit to LDP/Ca$h Presents. Send in the first three chapters, written or typed, of your completed manuscript to:

LDP: Submissions Dept
Po Box 944
Stockbridge, Ga 30281

DO NOT send original manuscript. Must be a duplicate.

Provide your synopsis and a cover letter containing your full contact information.

Thanks for considering LDP and Ca$h Presents.

NEW RELEASES

PROTÉGÉ OF A LEGEND 2 by COREY ROBINSON
BRONX SAVAGES by ROMELL TUKES
A GANGSTA'S PAIN 3 by J-BLUNT
THE STREETS NEVER LET GO 3 by ROBERT BAPTISTE
BODYMORE KINGPINS by ROMELL TUKES

Coming Soon from Lock Down Publications/Ca$h Presents

BLOOD OF A BOSS **VI**

SHADOWS OF THE GAME II

TRAP BASTARD II

By **Askari**

LOYAL TO THE GAME **IV**

By **T.J. & Jelissa**

TRUE SAVAGE **VIII**

MIDNIGHT CARTEL IV

DOPE BOY MAGIC IV

CITY OF KINGZ III

NIGHTMARE ON SILENT AVE II

THE PLUG OF LIL MEXICO II

CLASSIC CITY II

By **Chris Green**

BLAST FOR ME **III**

A SAVAGE DOPEBOY III

CUTTHROAT MAFIA III

DUFFLE BAG CARTEL VII

HEARTLESS GOON VI

By **Ghost**

A HUSTLER'S DECEIT III

KILL ZONE II

BAE BELONGS TO ME III

TIL DEATH II

By **Aryanna**

KING OF THE TRAP III

By **T.J. Edwards**

GORILLAZ IN THE BAY V

3X KRAZY III

STRAIGHT BEAST MODE III

De'Kari

KINGPIN KILLAZ IV

STREET KINGS III

PAID IN BLOOD III

CARTEL KILLAZ IV

DOPE GODS III

Hood Rich

SINS OF A HUSTLA II

ASAD

YAYO V

Bred In The Game 2

S. Allen

THE STREETS WILL TALK II

By Yolanda Moore

SON OF A DOPE FIEND III

HEAVEN GOT A GHETTO II

SKI MASK MONEY II

By Renta

LOYALTY AIN'T PROMISED III

By Keith Williams

I'M NOTHING WITHOUT HIS LOVE II

SINS OF A THUG II

TO THE THUG I LOVED BEFORE II

IN A HUSTLER I TRUST II

By Monet Dragun

QUIET MONEY IV

EXTENDED CLIP III

THUG LIFE IV

By **Trai'Quan**

THE STREETS MADE ME IV

By **Larry D. Wright**

IF YOU CROSS ME ONCE III

ANGEL V

By **Anthony Fields**

THE STREETS WILL NEVER CLOSE IV

By K'ajji

HARD AND RUTHLESS III

KILLA KOUNTY IV

By Khufu

MONEY GAME III

By Smoove Dolla

JACK BOYS VS DOPE BOYS IV

A GANGSTA'S QUR'AN V

COKE GIRLZ II

COKE BOYS II

LIFE OF A SAVAGE V

CHI'RAQ GANGSTAS V

SOSA GANG II

BRONX SAVAGES II

BODYMORE KINGPINS II

By Romell Tukes

MURDA WAS THE CASE III

Elijah R. Freeman

AN UNFORESEEN LOVE IV

BABY, I'M WINTERTIME COLD III

By **Meesha**

QUEEN OF THE ZOO III

By **Black Migo**

CONFESSIONS OF A JACKBOY III

By Nicholas Lock

GRIMEY WAYS III

By Ray Vinci

KING KILLA II

By Vincent "Vitto" Holloway

BETRAYAL OF A THUG III

By Fre$h

THE MURDER QUEENS III

By Michael Gallon

THE BIRTH OF A GANGSTER III

By Delmont Player

TREAL LOVE II

By Le'Monica Jackson

FOR THE LOVE OF BLOOD III

By Jamel Mitchell

RAN OFF ON DA PLUG II

By Paper Boi Rari

HOOD CONSIGLIERE III

By Keese

PRETTY GIRLS DO NASTY THINGS II

By Nicole Goosby

PROTÉGÉ OF A LEGEND III

By Corey Robinson

IT'S JUST ME AND YOU II

By Ah'Million

BORN IN THE GRAVE III

By Self Made Tay

FOREVER GANGSTA III

By Adrian Dulan

GORILLAZ IN THE TRENCHES II

By SayNoMore

THE COCAINE PRINCESS VII

By King Rio

CRIME BOSS II

Playa Ray

LOYALTY IS EVERYTHING III

Molotti

HERE TODAY GONE TOMORROW II

By Fly Rock

REAL G'S MOVE IN SILENCE II

By Von Diesel

Available Now

RESTRAINING ORDER **I & II**

By **CA$H & Coffee**

LOVE KNOWS NO BOUNDARIES **I II & III**

By **Coffee**

RAISED AS A GOON I, II, III & IV

BRED BY THE SLUMS I, II, III

BLAST FOR ME I & II

ROTTEN TO THE CORE I II III

A BRONX TALE I, II, III

DUFFLE BAG CARTEL I II III IV V VI

HEARTLESS GOON I II III IV V

A SAVAGE DOPEBOY I II

DRUG LORDS I II III

CUTTHROAT MAFIA I II

KING OF THE TRENCHES

By **Ghost**

LAY IT DOWN **I & II**

LAST OF A DYING BREED I II

BLOOD STAINS OF A SHOTTA I & II III

By **Jamaica**

LOYAL TO THE GAME I II III

LIFE OF SIN I, II III

By **TJ & Jelissa**

BLOODY COMMAS I & II

SKI MASK CARTEL I II & III

KING OF NEW YORK I II,III IV V

RISE TO POWER I II III

COKE KINGS I II III IV V

BORN HEARTLESS I II III IV

KING OF THE TRAP I II

By **T.J. Edwards**

IF LOVING HIM IS WRONG…I & II

LOVE ME EVEN WHEN IT HURTS I II III

By **Jelissa**

WHEN THE STREETS CLAP BACK I & II III

THE HEART OF A SAVAGE I II III IV

MONEY MAFIA I II

LOYAL TO THE SOIL I II III

By **Jibril Williams**

A DISTINGUISHED THUG STOLE MY HEART I II & III

LOVE SHOULDN'T HURT I II III IV

RENEGADE BOYS I II III IV

PAID IN KARMA I II III

SAVAGE STORMS I II III

AN UNFORESEEN LOVE I II III

BABY, I'M WINTERTIME COLD I II

By **Meesha**

A GANGSTER'S CODE I &, II III

A GANGSTER'S SYN I II III

THE SAVAGE LIFE I II III

CHAINED TO THE STREETS I II III

BLOOD ON THE MONEY I II III

A GANGSTA'S PAIN I II III

By J-Blunt

PUSH IT TO THE LIMIT

By **Bre' Hayes**

BLOOD OF A BOSS **I, II, III, IV, V**

SHADOWS OF THE GAME

TRAP BASTARD

By **Askari**

THE STREETS BLEED MURDER **I, II & III**

THE HEART OF A GANGSTA I II& III

By **Jerry Jackson**

CUM FOR ME I II III IV V VI VII VIII

An **LDP Erotica Collaboration**

BRIDE OF A HUSTLA **I II & II**

THE FETTI GIRLS **I, II& III**

CORRUPTED BY A GANGSTA I, II III, IV

BLINDED BY HIS LOVE

THE PRICE YOU PAY FOR LOVE I, II ,III

DOPE GIRL MAGIC I II III

By **Destiny Skai**

WHEN A GOOD GIRL GOES BAD

By **Adrienne**

THE COST OF LOYALTY I II III

By Kweli

A GANGSTER'S REVENGE **I II III & IV**

THE BOSS MAN'S DAUGHTERS I II III IV V

A SAVAGE LOVE **I & II**

BAE BELONGS TO ME I II

A HUSTLER'S DECEIT I, II, III

WHAT BAD BITCHES DO I, II, III

SOUL OF A MONSTER I II III

KILL ZONE

A DOPE BOY'S QUEEN I II III

TIL DEATH

By **Aryanna**

A KINGPIN'S AMBITON

A KINGPIN'S AMBITION **II**

I MURDER FOR THE DOUGH

By **Ambitious**

TRUE SAVAGE I II III IV V VI VII

DOPE BOY MAGIC I, II, III

MIDNIGHT CARTEL I II III

CITY OF KINGZ I II

NIGHTMARE ON SILENT AVE

THE PLUG OF LIL MEXICO II

CLASSIC CITY

By **Chris Green**

A DOPEBOY'S PRAYER

By **Eddie "Wolf" Lee**

THE KING CARTEL **I, II & III**

By **Frank Gresham**

THESE NIGGAS AIN'T LOYAL **I, II & III**

By **Nikki Tee**

GANGSTA SHYT **I II &III**

By **CATO**

THE ULTIMATE BETRAYAL

By **Phoenix**

BOSS'N UP **I , II & III**

By **Royal Nicole**

I LOVE YOU TO DEATH

By **Destiny J**

I RIDE FOR MY HITTA

I STILL RIDE FOR MY HITTA

By **Misty Holt**

LOVE & CHASIN' PAPER

By **Qay Crockett**

TO DIE IN VAIN

SINS OF A HUSTLA

By **ASAD**

BROOKLYN HUSTLAZ

By **Boogsy Morina**

BROOKLYN ON LOCK I & II

By **Sonovia**

GANGSTA CITY

By **Teddy Duke**

A DRUG KING AND HIS DIAMOND I & II III

A DOPEMAN'S RICHES

HER MAN, MINE'S TOO I, II

CASH MONEY HO'S

THE WIFEY I USED TO BE I II

PRETTY GIRLS DO NASTY THINGS

By Nicole Goosby

TRAPHOUSE KING **I II & III**

KINGPIN KILLAZ I II III

STREET KINGS I II

PAID IN BLOOD **I II**

CARTEL KILLAZ I II III

DOPE GODS I II

By **Hood Rich**

LIPSTICK KILLAH **I, II, III**

CRIME OF PASSION I II & III

FRIEND OR FOE I II III

By **Mimi**

STEADY MOBBN' **I, II, III**

THE STREETS STAINED MY SOUL I II III

By **Marcellus Allen**

WHO SHOT YA **I, II, III**

SON OF A DOPE FIEND I II

HEAVEN GOT A GHETTO

SKI MASK MONEY

Renta

GORILLAZ IN THE BAY **I II III IV**

TEARS OF A GANGSTA I II

3X KRAZY I II

STRAIGHT BEAST MODE I II

DE'KARI

TRIGGADALE I II III

MURDAROBER WAS THE CASE I II

Elijah R. Freeman

GOD BLESS THE TRAPPERS I, II, III

THESE SCANDALOUS STREETS I, II, III

FEAR MY GANGSTA I, II, III IV, V

THESE STREETS DON'T LOVE NOBODY I, II

BURY ME A G I, II, III, IV, V

A GANGSTA'S EMPIRE I, II, III, IV

THE DOPEMAN'S BODYGAURD I II

THE REALEST KILLAZ I II III

THE LAST OF THE OGS I II III

Tranay Adams

THE STREETS ARE CALLING

Duquie Wilson

MARRIED TO A BOSS I II III

By Destiny Skai & Chris Green

KINGZ OF THE GAME I II III IV V VI

CRIME BOSS

Playa Ray

SLAUGHTER GANG I II III

RUTHLESS HEART I II III

By Willie Slaughter

FUK SHYT

By Blakk Diamond

DON'T F#CK WITH MY HEART I II

By Linnea

ADDICTED TO THE DRAMA I II III

IN THE ARM OF HIS BOSS II

By Jamila

YAYO I II III IV

A SHOOTER'S AMBITION I II

BRED IN THE GAME

By S. Allen

TRAP GOD I II III

RICH $AVAGE I II III

MONEY IN THE GRAVE I II III

By Martell Troublesome Bolden

FOREVER GANGSTA I II

GLOCKS ON SATIN SHEETS I II

By Adrian Dulan

TOE TAGZ I II III IV

LEVELS TO THIS SHYT I II

IT'S JUST ME AND YOU

By Ah'Million

KINGPIN DREAMS I II III

RAN OFF ON DA PLUG

By Paper Boi Rari

CONFESSIONS OF A GANGSTA I II III IV

CONFESSIONS OF A JACKBOY I II

By Nicholas Lock

I'M NOTHING WITHOUT HIS LOVE

SINS OF A THUG

TO THE THUG I LOVED BEFORE

A GANGSTA SAVED XMAS

IN A HUSTLER I TRUST

By Monet Dragun

CAUGHT UP IN THE LIFE I II III

THE STREETS NEVER LET GO I II III

By Robert Baptiste

NEW TO THE GAME I II III

MONEY, MURDER & MEMORIES I II III

By **Malik D. Rice**

LIFE OF A SAVAGE I II III IV

A GANGSTA'S QUR'AN I II III IV

MURDA SEASON I II III

GANGLAND CARTEL I II III

CHI'RAQ GANGSTAS I II III IV

KILLERS ON ELM STREET I II III

JACK BOYZ N DA BRONX I II III

A DOPEBOY'S DREAM I II III

JACK BOYS VS DOPE BOYS I II III

COKE GIRLZ

COKE BOYS

SOSA GANG

BRONX SAVAGES

BODYMORE KINGPINS

By Romell Tukes

LOYALTY AIN'T PROMISED I II

By Keith Williams

QUIET MONEY I II III

THUG LIFE I II III

EXTENDED CLIP I II

A GANGSTA'S PARADISE

By **Trai'Quan**

THE STREETS MADE ME I II III

By **Larry D. Wright**

THE ULTIMATE SACRIFICE I, II, III, IV, V, VI

KHADIFI

IF YOU CROSS ME ONCE I II

ANGEL I II III IV

IN THE BLINK OF AN EYE

By **Anthony Fields**

THE LIFE OF A HOOD STAR

By Ca$h & Rashia Wilson

THE STREETS WILL NEVER CLOSE I II III

By K'ajji

CREAM I II III

THE STREETS WILL TALK

By Yolanda Moore

NIGHTMARES OF A HUSTLA I II III

By King Dream

CONCRETE KILLA I II III

VICIOUS LOYALTY I II III

By Kingpen

HARD AND RUTHLESS I II

MOB TOWN 251

THE BILLIONAIRE BENTLEYS I II III

REAL G'S MOVE IN SILENCE

By Von Diesel

GHOST MOB

Stilloan Robinson

MOB TIES I II III IV V VI

SOUL OF A HUSTLER, HEART OF A KILLER I II

GORILLAZ IN THE TRENCHES

By SayNoMore

BODYMORE MURDERLAND I II III

THE BIRTH OF A GANGSTER I II

By Delmont Player

FOR THE LOVE OF A BOSS

By C. D. Blue

MOBBED UP I II III IV

THE BRICK MAN I II III IV V

THE COCAINE PRINCESS I II III IV V VI

By King Rio

KILLA KOUNTY I II III IV

By Khufu

MONEY GAME I II

By Smoove Dolla

A GANGSTA'S KARMA I II III

By FLAME

KING OF THE TRENCHES I II III

by **GHOST & TRANAY ADAMS**

QUEEN OF THE ZOO I II

By **Black Migo**

GRIMEY WAYS I II

By Ray Vinci

XMAS WITH AN ATL SHOOTER

By Ca$h & Destiny Skai

KING KILLA

By Vincent "Vitto" Holloway

BETRAYAL OF A THUG I II

By Fre$h

THE MURDER QUEENS I II

By Michael Gallon

TREAL LOVE

By Le'Monica Jackson

FOR THE LOVE OF BLOOD I II

By Jamel Mitchell

HOOD CONSIGLIERE I II

By Keese

PROTÉGÉ OF A LEGEND I II

By Corey Robinson

BORN IN THE GRAVE I II

By Self Made Tay

MOAN IN MY MOUTH

By XTASY

TORN BETWEEN A GANGSTER AND A GENTLEMAN

By J-BLUNT & Miss Kim

LOYALTY IS EVERYTHING I II

Molotti

HERE TODAY GONE TOMORROW

By Fly Rock

PILLOW PRINCESS

By S. Hawkins

BOOKS BY LDP'S CEO, CA$H

TRUST IN NO MAN

TRUST IN NO MAN 2

TRUST IN NO MAN 3

BONDED BY BLOOD

SHORTY GOT A THUG

THUGS CRY

THUGS CRY 2

THUGS CRY 3

TRUST NO BITCH

TRUST NO BITCH 2

TRUST NO BITCH 3

TIL MY CASKET DROPS

RESTRAINING ORDER

RESTRAINING ORDER 2

IN LOVE WITH A CONVICT

LIFE OF A HOOD STAR

XMAS WITH AN ATL SHOOTER

CPSIA information can be obtained
at www.ICGtesting.com
Printed in the USA
LVHW041834240223
740361LV00001B/87

9 781958 111840